This
Terrestrial
Hell

Kevin Quigley

This Terrestrial Hell

Kevin Quigley

CEMETERY DANCE PUBLICATIONS

Baltimore
❖ 2018 ❖

FIRST U.S. EDITION
ISBN: 978-1-58767-488-4
Cemetery Dance Publications First Edition 2018

Cemetery Dance Publications
132-B Industry Lane, Unit 7
Forest Hill, MD 21050
Email: info@cemeterydance.com
www.cemeterydance.com

Table of Contents

"Night in the Doghouse"   9
"Helminthos"   27
"Baby, It's Cold Outside"   43
"Funhouse Frank and His Zodiac Freaks"   65
"Quarry Story"   83
"Screw You"   113
"The Curious Life of Dennis Morbach"   121
"The Fear is in Tents"   133
"Busting Heavies"   143
"Last Night at the Bear"   161
"La Fenêtre du Grenier"   173

"Kill them," my training said. "Everyone kills them. It's a public service." My finger moved to the trigger. The cross was steady on the breast just below the panting tongue. I could imagine the splash and jar of angry steel, the leap and struggle until the torn heart failed, and then, not too long later, the shadow of a buzzard, and another... And beside the sagebush there would be a naked, eyeless skull, a few picked bones, a spot of black dried blood, and a few rags of golden fur.

–John Steinbeck,
Travels With Charley: In Search of America

For David Mogolov and Delbert Marr, who read these stories and told me how to make them better.

And for my dad.

Night in the Doghouse

Crash!

"Jesus," Mary said, shaken. A sudden blue flash of light illuminated her face, strobing it in a fiery quick-freeze. She looked over at Hank, who, for a moment, seemed scared himself. Then, the lightning retracted, and she could only see him in the reflected glow of the headlights cutting through the rain.

"Yeah, kind of close, huh?" Hank agreed, chuckling nervously.

"Hank, why don't we just find a motel somewhere? Get out of the rain, get warm." She tried to sound casual.

"We can make it to Roger and Jean's tonight," he answered, wiping his arm across his side of the windshield. Silence fell between them. The radio, which had come in intermittently for the past half hour or so, was now off. She knew he could see her looking at him through the corner of his eye, but wasn't acknowledging her. It always frustrated her when he acted like this.

"Hank."

"Yeah, hon?" His tone was abrupt, annoyed.

"Roger and Jean live over a hundred miles away. Even under best conditions, it would take us almost two hours to get there."

"We'll get there."

"There you go again. Stubborn, macho Hank."

"Mary, no one says 'macho' anymore." He glanced at her, a small smile on his face, then turned back to the road, squinting. There was a large, dark form up ahead and to the right: a large house with its lights turned off. They both glanced forward at it with mild surprise. It was the first house they'd seen for miles. Then, remembering his comment, she said, "Now that you've had the smug satisfaction of correcting my slang usage, perhaps we could find a motel."

"Mary, we're making good time."

"We're *making*," she began, pointing to the odometer, "Thirty miles an hour. It's pitch black, it's raining, and it's almost ten o'clock. It won't kill us to get there tomorrow morning."

"Roger's taking us to breakfast at ten in the morning. He's already made reservations. And I'd like to get a chess game in with him before we eat. If we stop now, we'll have to get up early and hurry there, and you know how cranky you get when you have to wake up early."

"*Me*? Look who's—Hank, look out!"

Hank shot his eyes toward the road. Just in time, he saw his headlights catch the dog standing on the pavement; first his headlights, then his bumper. The dog flew up in a crazy arc, landing too far away to see in the driving sheets of rain.

Mary yelped as Hank stamped on the brake pedal. The tires were wet and squealed, skidding almost a foot before the car came to a halt. Mary and Hank exchanged wide-eyed glances.

Mary asked, "Do you think it's dead?"

"I don't know," Hank answered. Mary heard a shaky uncertainty in his voice.

A moment passed, silent but for the metallic sound of rain battering the roof. "Go check," Mary said suddenly, breaking them both from their reverie.

He turned, maybe to argue or refute or accuse, but only nodded. It was the right thing to do.

She watched as Hank stepped through his door, then a surge of almost maternal protectiveness swept over her. She didn't like seeing him enter that dark night alone. After a slight hesitation, she gripped her own door handle and followed him out into the rain.

It was icy and unyielding. Pinpricks of sharp rain bit into her head, neck, and back. It was mid-May in western Massachusetts, late enough for the rain to have heated to tolerable levels, but not tonight. Tonight, the rain embodied the cold, sucking warmth from her like a giant heat-vampire. She trembled and shook in little spasms, making her way to the front of the car.

The twin beams of light had placed the dog easily. It lay in an unnatural sprawl, its blood black in the night, pooling around it, then diluting and flowing away in the rain. Hank was kneeling beside the animal, rain soaking his clothes and falling in little streams from his ears and nose. She watched as the dog hitched one shuddery breath, and then its side fell, not rising again.

"Oh God, Hank," she said, kneeling across from him. Two of the dog's legs had fractured, bending in bizarre, misshapen positions. A third had snapped of, and in the halogen glow, Mary could see a bright white glint of bone poking from what remained of its thigh. She held back her gorge, glancing up to look away from the dog, as if the very sight of it would singe her eyes. She thought of the house, the black silhouette against the angry sky, looming large on a back country road that couldn't claim another house for at least twenty miles. If the dog wasn't a stray, it was a good assumption that it had come from the house.

As if reading her thoughts, Hank said, "We should bring it up to the house." He looked at her, and she saw there was a vague sort of fear in his eyes. She recognized it because she felt the same fear, but couldn't put a face on it. It just sat there, hunched in her stomach, and she didn't know why.

Hastily, she nodded. "I'll get the blanket from the back seat." She returned with it a minute later, then looked to the side of the road.

"Kind of hard to even see the house, isn't it?"

He squinted, looking. "It's there. Can I have the blanket?" She handed it to him just as another sear of lightning tattooed the sky, brightening the dark road. The house seemed to materialize in front of them like an apparition, very close to where they stood.

"I see it now. Kind of dark, huh?" She hoped she kept the tremble out of her voice.

"It's late," he said, and set about wrapping the dog in the afghan, a gift from Mary's late grandmother.

"Maybe they don't want us waking them up."

"Maybe they'd like to know their dog is in several pieces in the road."

A pause.

"Then I'm coming with you."

"You can watch the car, hon. I'll only be a few minutes."

Fear crept into her heart, fear she could not articulate. Again, that maternal instinct kicked in, the need to protect him even if he did not want it. She didn't want him to go up to that dark house alone.

Mary said none of these things. "It's not you I'm worried about. I'm more concerned with the potential slaughter that seems to happen to young, pretty girls left alone on deserted roads."

It was an old joke between them, and Hank tried a strained grin in the ghostly glow of the headlights. "I got pretty, but what's this about young?"

"I'm scared, Hank. I know that sounds all girly but I am."

"Nothing girly about it. It's plenty spooky out here, I'll give you that. Okay, come on. Let's get this over with."

They bundled the animal into the blanket, and made their way toward the porch. Mary began to feel that unplaced fear resurface. Her comment had been meant as a joke, but it was late, and anything could happen in the dark. Could this really be the only house for twenty miles? Or more?

After mounting the steps to the porch, Mary stumbling a bit on her end of the weight, they put the dog down and looked solemnly at the front door. Lightning came again, and Mary saw a glint of metal by the side of the house. Looking around, she spotted the dark hulks of two or three cars rotting in the tall grass. She grinned smugly. *Hick country*, she thought.

"This is going to be hard," Hank whispered to her. "What if this is a little kid's dog? Or some old guy's seeing eye dog? God, this sucks." Hank breathed in, exhaled, and nodded to himself. Leaning out, he rapped lightly on the door. They waited. A few minutes ticked by, and the rain got heavier.

"Maybe you should knock a little harder," Mary said, looking down at the porch where the dead dog lay. Her unease sharpened now. Fear pervaded. The idea of a motel seemed like heaven to her now, and she was sure that after this debacle, she could talk her husband into it.

Hank knocked again, and when a full minute passed, he pounded. Nothing.

"Honey," Mary began, "Maybe we should just leave..." Then, the door opened. Hank and Mary Garber looked down and saw a young girl of about eight. She had long, scraggly blond hair and thick glasses which enlarged her pale blue eyes. Dirty blue jeans clung to her legs, and a simple, disheveled pink blouse covered her top. The girl looked at the adult couple for a moment, then down at the blanket on the porch.

"L-little girl," Hank began, "Is your mommy or daddy home?"

The girl looked again at the blanket, her eyes growing wider. "Oh my God," she said in a small voice. She appeared to be near the edge of tears. "Oh my God, not again." Mary stared at her. Something that was not quite sadness showed in the girl's eyes. Could it be... was that fear?

The girl glanced up, shooting her gaze first at Mary, then Hank. She shuffled out onto the porch in an almost elderly manner and shut the door quietly behind her. Somewhere in the distance, thunder growled ominously.

"You have to go," the girl said quietly, in a conspiratorial tone. "Please, just leave the..." She broke off, looked uneasily back at the door leading into the house, and turned back to them. "Just leave it, and drive away. Fast."

"Sweetie, what's wrong?" Mary asked. Now, the previously dormant maternal instinct rose up inside her with a vengeance, a need to protect this girl. From what, she didn't know, but by the look of this downtrodden, scared little girl, it was something bad.

"Nothing's wrong." But her eyes betrayed her. Mary saw that her eyes begged for help.

"Are your mom and dad asleep?" Hank persisted, bewildered. The girl looked up at him sharply.

"No!" she cried, and though her voice registered little over a whisper, she clasped her hands to her mouth and her eyes shot glances into the rain.

"Where are they?" Mary asked, speaking calmly and keeping her voice as low as the girl's. The blonde girl looked up into Mary's rain-streaked face, into her eyes, and began to cry.

Mary grabbed the girl and hugged her close. She could feel the girl's heat against her legs even through the rain and the denim. After a few moments, she bent down and asked, "What about your parents?"

"They... they'll hurt me." The girl was struggling with the words. She seemed to be on the brink of telling them something, but unsure of whether she should. Mary saw hysteria creep into her eyes.

"Okay, clam down," Mary said soothingly. "What's your name?"

"A-April." Then, as an afterthought, "Lansing."

"Okay, April, where are your parents?"

"They're in the cellar." The girl's face contorted.

Hank, his own face a mixture of confusion and fear, bent down to the girl and asked, "What are they doing in the cellar?"

April's composure broke apart. Her voice jumped up to a scream, louder than the driving rain. "They're dead! They're dead and so is my little brother Devin! *They* killed him! *They* keep me here!" Wide-eyed and using the last of her breath, April screamed even louder, "*And you just killed one of them!*"

Thunder rumbled. Mary, terrified, looked up at Hank.

"Let's get out of here, Hank. We'll take her with us. Let's go." She grabbed Hank by the shirt and the girl by the hand and began to walk toward the steps.

"Mary, we can't just leave here. The girl's parents…"

"She says they're dead, Hank. Do you want to wait around for whoever did it to kill us?"

Hank looked at April. "What do you mean we killed one of them?"

April began to answer, then seemed to spot something over Mary's hunched shoulder. She began to shriek.

"They're outside! They're coming!"

Both Hank and Mary turned to look. Two pairs of golden eyes, low to the muddy ground, stared up at them. Vague outlines surrounded the eyes: compact, perhaps muscular bodies. But Mary and Hank only saw the teeth. Two huge, gaping sets of jaws opened and then clamped shut. Rainwater crashed from the jaws like burst membranes.

Now it was Hank's turn to pull. He grabbed Mary in one arm and April in the other and huddled them toward the door. The knob was slick, hard to turn. A low, guttural moan threatened from behind, and it sounded close.

"Turn, Hank, *turn!*" Mary shrieked. Then, the door flew open, and they were inside. Hank slammed the door shut in time to hear two giant thumps from the other side. All three of them screamed.

The room was bathed in darkness. The only light that entered was from a small semicircular window at the top of the door they stood against, and a window set into the far wall. Otherwise, pure black.

April began hitching in short, rapid breaths. She looked as if she were trying to scream, but the scream was too great for her small throat. Only a small, choked sound escaped: ug, ug, ug.

Seemingly without provocation, Hank reached back his arm and slapped the girl across the face. April's scream came then, high and piercing.

"Hank, don't!"

"She was going to hyperventilate," Hank answered her distractedly. His gaze focused on April. "Were those dogs out there?"

She stopped screaming abruptly and nodded emphatically.

"Is it... is it dogs that keep you here?"

April nodded again, more dramatically this time.

"Dogs?" Mary asked from behind him. "Just dogs?"

"*Not* just dogs!" April yelled at them. The room they stood in now seemed bigger in the black; April's words echoed and bounced off of far, unseen walls. "*Freak*-dogs. That's what Devin called them. Freak-dogs. And then they *killed* him!"

"Jesus," Hank muttered. He began to glance back at the door, afraid there might be another way in.

"One of them ran out in front of our car. Mommy and Daddy were taking us on vacation, up to Maine. That's when we hit the dog. We brought it up to the house." Her voice hitched again, and she seemed to fight to regain some composure. "They circled around," April continued. "They bit. My mommy and daddy wanted to leave after Devin... just after. And the freak-dogs bit at them. Mommy started to bleed and my dad tried to kill one of them with a chair. Then they killed them, too." The girl began to cry again, but had apparently expended all her energy. "I guess they moved the car out back with the others. I don't know how. Now they just keep me here. There are cans of food in the cellar. The dogs can't open them, so they keep me."

Mary stood up, squinting to see into the dark room. Not much light filtered in, from either window above and behind them or the one at the far end of the room. Here, darkness persisted, and anything could be keeping company with them.

A terrifying thought occurred to her.

"April, how many dogs are there?"

April didn't have a chance to answer. From somewhere in the dark, Mary heard a rapid clack-clack advancing: the sound of sharp toenails on hard wood. Before she could do anything, she saw a huge, outstretched figure leap into their semi-light. An angry, howling sound filled the room, echoing off unseen walls and ceilings. Mary watched as huge, meaty paws landed on the girl's shoulders from behind. A gigantic set of jaws clamped down on her head, biting into her small skull and tearing. Her glasses flew off, crashing to the floor somewhere in the room's immense darkness. Blood spurted from April's forehead and darkened her blond hair. As the girl screamed again, another set of jaws clamped down on her throat, ripping the sound from her. They brought her to the ground, and for a moment, Mary and Hank were stunned to numbness by the sight.

What looked like a pit bull terrier and a Rottweiler were tearing the little blonde girl to pieces in front of them. In the half-darkness Mary saw super-fast jaws dart into the light and tear a chunk of meat and clothing away. The girl's face was hidden in the shadows beyond them.

The dogs seemed to have no interest in them at the moment. Mary tried to make her legs run somewhere, anywhere. They refused to go.

Another flash of teeth. The girl's arm ripped off with a disgustingly moist sound.

"Move, move, move," Hank whispered, and then she heard him throwing up. For some reason, that sound, real in all this lunacy, broke her paralysis. Still holding Hank's hand, she bolted into the dark, dark room.

Darkness enclosed them on all sides. They could still hear the sounds of eating from behind them, but that was best not to think about. The girl was dead, and they had to get out of here. The two large dogs blocked the way they came in, but there had to be another way out. This room itself seemed to be huge; they had been running—actually running—for twenty seconds or more and were still encased in dark, the shadows of the room becoming almost tangible. The rain pounded on the windows like a threat. Mary was on the verge of shrieking, holding it down only because she was terrified of being joined by others.

"The kitchen," Hank said suddenly, pulling her to the left. "I think I see a door!"

"Hank!" Mary stage-whispered. "How do you know that's the kitchen? There could be anything in there!" She was now on the verge of hysterics, keeping only the barest of senses about her. She would not scream, not this girl, no way.

"It's got to be better than what we just saw!" She couldn't argue with his logic, not in this panic state. Allowing her arm to be pulled, she followed him to the far left side of the room, the edges of a door just barely visible in the dim light cast by the outside window. Suddenly, a flash of lightning danced merrily outside, blinding, the walls visible in a brief and intense burst of light. Mary glanced around the gigantic room, terrified. Dozens—maybe hundreds—of large, dark animals loomed in the corners and huddled by the walls. Their eyes shone glassily in the blue-yellow light. From all around, almost drowning in the sound of the pouring rain, was a low, guttural growl. A *hungry* growl.

Now, Mary *did* scream, a loud, curdling knife cutting into the renewed darkness. She heaved forward, pushing Hank into the door. It swung open freely on spring hinges, allowing them through, then closing back into place. Mary thought briefly, *That door swings open. Any of those dogs can get in. Any of them.* The image of the pit bull's attack on April momentarily buzzed into her mind, but it was gone when she looked into this new room.

Hank had been right: it was a kitchen. Several candles, presumably lit by April, stood on countertops and the top of the large stove on the far side of the room. The walls had been tiled in white and yellow, the floor in a nondescript shade of linoleum.

Dogs were everywhere.

All of them were small dogs. A white and brown Jack Russell terrier stood on a chair, its paws on the large wooden table in front of it, eating some slop off of a plate. To Mary, it looked like a contestant in a pie-eating contest. Other dogs, Mary didn't know which breeds, half-sat, half-stood around the table in similar fashion, and for a crazy, surreal moment, Mary thought of that old picture of dogs playing poker. The image made her want to laugh hysterically, laugh until no sound came out, but she finally suppressed it.

Several cans of DogDish dog food stood stacked by the end of the table, unopened. Mary saw a can opener, one of the old manual kinds, lying near the cans. It caught glints of the candlelight on its metallic surface, sparkling into the dark room. A tiny Chihuahua stood sentry by the cans, pacing back and forth, staring at the two newcomers. It shook minutely, as if it were excited, its ears standing at attention. Mary found that, even with the rain beating against the windows, she could still hear its tiny claws clicking against the wood of the table. If she had to listen to that much longer, she felt she would go insane.

A sad-looking basset hound and a Welsh corgi were playing tug-of-war with something by the legs of the table. As Mary looked closer, she saw with muted anguish that it was a man's severed hand. Two miniature dachshunds stood stoically by a door set into the back wall, their long, cylindrical bodies low to the floor, like watchmen at Fort Knox. In the corner, a Scotty dog and a poodle were wrestling playfully. None of the dogs seemed to care much about their presence, with the possible exception of the Chihuahua, who seemed to have a vague suspicion in its eyes.

"Mary," Hank whispered to her, breaking her near-panic.

"What?" She was panting. *Like a dog*, she thought crazily, *panting like a dog.*

"There's a door over there." He paused, swallowing. Mary caught a glimpse of his face, horrified, in the dancing candlelight. Even in this terrible situation, he was trying to be the protector, the hero. In a moment, she loved him and feared for them both. Because one wrong move could get them both killed.

Like April, she thought, and shuddered.

"I think that the door there leads outside. If we can just get out there, I'm pretty sure we can get to the car, and get the hell out of here."

"That's a lot of I thinks and pretty sures," Mary shot back, her voice cracking as she tried to keep it down to a whisper.

Still, most of the dogs hadn't paid attention to them, but she thought she saw one of the dachshunds twitch its nose in their direction.

"You wanna stay here?" Hank asked, sounding angry, but Mary heard the fear creep into his voice. "You wanna be dessert for the ones who munched on the little girl out there? Huh?" His voice rose steadily in a hyper pitch. Now, a lot of the dogs were noticing them. The basset hound and the corgi had dropped the hand, and now it lay between them on the linoleum like a scar.

"Let's go," she said, and moved when he did toward the door. They had almost reached it, and the guarding dachshunds, when the barking began.

It was the Jack Russell. Mary whirled around to see it. The dog had finished its plate of mashed dog chow and now stood on the table, staring at them with black, black eyes. It had hunched down, its teeth bared, its ears sharp and pointed back in anger. It seemed to be pointing at them, at the only humans here, like an arrow of accusation. And it started to bark again: *Yyyyip! Yyyip! Yip-yip-yip-yip-yip!*

The Chihuahua joined in, followed by the screech of the poodle and the low, moaning howl of the beagle. And she began to hear other barks as well; they came from above her, around her, behind her. The sound of dogs barking filled the world, and Mary remembered in a blind flash of terror that the swinging door to the kitchen had been left unattended, and that there were *big* dogs out there.

"Go, Hank!" she screamed, pushing him from behind, the panic swirling in her mind like bees. "Go, go!"

They reached the door and Hank had just grasped the handle, when the dachshunds looked up at him. Mary had a second to see the murderous loathing in their eyes before they jumped simultaneously, latching onto Hank's arm and writhing.

The others came at lightning speed. The poodle, yipping the entire way, sped across the room and sunk its teeth into one of Hank's legs through his jeans. The beagle bit into his other leg, lower and toward the ankle. Hank began screaming, a high, girlish shriek, and it was only then that Mary realized she was also screaming.

In two solid jumps, the Jack Russell had leapt from the table to the floor, and from the floor to the stove. It watched intently as the other small dogs bit at Hank, as if calculating its next move. Growling, it then pushed off from the stove and latched its jaws into Hank's cheek. Hank stumbled backward, then toppled to the floor.

The terrier lunged forward with its jaws, gnashing and biting. A hunk of muscle and flesh came off in its teeth, the dog shaking it furiously as if to rid it of some foul taste.

A hunk of Hank, Mary thought, and suddenly, her hysterical laughter joined the barks of the dogs.

Racing to join the feast, the corgi leapt on Hank's chest and began tearing his still-moist T-shirt to shreds with its teeth. Without further announcement, it began tearing Hank's stomach to shreds. Blood jetted everywhere, spraying the white stove with a mist of red and matting the dogs' fur down to their bodies.

The Chihuahua darted at Hank's neck, entering the flesh around his Adam's apple and then tearing it out. At some point during the attack, Hank had stopped screaming.

Mary, on some vague level, now understood two things. One, the dogs weren't touching her; and two, the door Hank had been reaching for was now unoccupied. Hank had fallen into the kitchen, not toward the wall, and she could easily slip through, and out, and into freedom.

The frenzy continued. She saw herself leap forward, over Hank's now decimated legs, and her hand went to the doorknob. It wouldn't turn at first, but that was because her palm was slick with sweat. She tightened her grip, turned, and yanked.

It didn't lead outside. It was dark there, and there was a steep stairwell, leading down.

To the cellar.

Mary turned back, glimpsing the wreck that her husband had become in the split-second before she saw the swinging door explode inward. A gigantic gray dog bounded toward her, snarling and growling. Dog spit trailed out from its muzzle in a whitish stream. Its eyes were wild, reflecting fire from the candle flame. The growl erupting from its throat seemed huge, booming like a commando's charging battle cry. She even recognized what it was, because she'd had a dog like this when she was a little girl. It was a Siberian husky, and as she remembered, it was one strong dog.

It charged at her. She found her feet planted in the doorway. Paralyzed, she watched the dog project itself off the ground, slamming its bullet head into her stomach. She felt herself falling backward, and she knew even before she connected that she wouldn't be hitting the floor like Hank had. Because there were stairs behind her.

Backward and down, topsy-turvy, heels over head. The world became a chaotic jumble, the angry, hungry faces of freak-dogs in every reverse tumble. Finally, she felt her back strike a solid, horizontal surface; a floor. She kept her eyes tightly closed, but she sensed through her membranes in her eyelids that there was more light here, probably more candles. She could hear nothing. It was the smell that forced her to open her eyes, though, the smell of moldy, festering putrescence. The smell of black rot.

Her eyes fluttered open. Standing above her, and in her view upside-down, was the Siberian husky. In its jaws it held a bloody Converse sneaker. Hank's sneaker. Hank's foot was still in it. A white shard of bone shone in the candlelight down here, poking up from the skin and muscle just above Hank's ankle. A drop of blood pattered down onto her face and she screamed. She screamed until her throat felt as if it would burst, and then she continued to scream. The scream carried her down into blackness, into a faint so deep there were no dogs.

* * *

Mary awoke an unknown time later, disoriented and hoarse. It only took her a moment to remember where she was. The smell rushed back into her nostrils and she gagged. The sound seemed to entice the circle of dogs that stood around her, snarling. She sat up quickly, terror trying to creep into her mind, but she staved it back. They weren't advancing on her, at least. Not yet, anyway.

One dog, a Dalmatian, broke from the circle. It came to her, trotting, and took the tail of her shirt in its mouth. It tugged forward, not tearing the fabric, but it seemed insistent. It wanted her to go with it.

Slowly, she stood, quickly surveying the dogs. Boxers, bulldogs, Rottweilers, and Saint Bernards all stood in the loose circle. She couldn't make a break for it or they'd tear her apart in seconds. Better for now to just do what they wanted.

The Dalmatian led her to a door flanked on both sides by large, columnar candles. They were almost like the type of ceremonial candles she saw in church. The smell grew stronger here, and Mary had to hold back her gorge, pausing. The dog at her shirt tugged gently again, urging her to open the door. She reached forward slowly, and turned the knob.

She was violently ill for a moment. The stench rolled out, bombarding her, and she heaved before she even saw the source. Six corpses in various stages of decay littered the ground inside the room. Three men, two women, and one small child. Mary remembered April saying the dogs killed her family, her mom and dad and her little brother Devin.

Freak-dogs, April had told them, before the girl and Mary's husband joined the ranks of the dead, *that's what my little brother Devin called them. Then they killed him.*

The other woman and one of the men might have been the original owners of the house. The other man was dressed in the remains of a business suit. It didn't matter. They were all dead now.

The bodies, however, were overshadowed by the real contents of the small room: hundreds upon hundreds of cans of DogDish dog food. Their metal tops glimmered in the flickering lights.

Mary heard a small sound at her feet. It was the Chihuahua, holding the manual can opener in its tiny teeth. It stretched out its head, bringing the can opener closer to her fingers.

It's a trade-off, Mary thought, her eyes wide with fear, *The dog food for my life. They feed, or they kill. And they never bite the hand that feeds them, unless there's someone else there to take up the slack.*

Trembling, she took the can opener. Outside, she could hear the steady whir of a car's motor. Their car. Somehow, the dogs were moving it off the road and to the side of the house, next to the other car husks, to rot like the bodies in this room.

"How long are you going to keep me?" she asked, her voice wavering. "Until the next traveler runs down one of your kamikaze friends? Or what about if and when the police find our car, or someone else's? How long, freak-dogs?" She choked on the last word, a tear falling to the floor.

The Dalmatian and the Chihuahua began to growl softly, in unison, and Mary heard an echo of the girl's words: *And then they killed him.*

She went to the cans, crying in terror, and began opening.

Helminthos

I was seven years old when I first met Larry Brahms. That was fifteen years ago, when things made more sense than they do now... and when I didn't wake up in the middle of the night, screaming into the dark.

Larry's parents moved into my neighborhood from some small town out west. His dad was some vague type of businessman for a big company whose name I still don't know. One day, my mom ran into his mom at the supermarket, and both of them were delighted to find that their boys had someone their own age to play with. When Mom told me, I was pretty excited myself. My neighborhood—a sleepy little street that ended in a similarly sleepy little cul-de-sac—was packed with either geriatrics or happy young couples with squalling infants. I could read or play with BJ, my dog, but after a while, you sort of craved human connection. The thought of Larry offered hope.

One hot summer day, his mom arrived with him in tow; he tried his best to hide behind her, but I wasn't having any of it. I stepped right up and stuck out my hand. "Hi!" I shouted. "My name's Dennis! What's your name?"

His mom was shaking her head. "Larry's a little bit shy, Dennis. He probably won't..."

But then he did. He peeked out from behind his mother, his tiny, shy little eyes exploring my face, then reached out his own tentative hand. "I'm Larry," he said to me. "Larry Brahms. You're nice."

His mom seemed astonished. I heard her say to my mom, "Larry's never responded that quickly to a person before. He..."

And that's when all hell broke loose.

Probably sensing that there was new blood in the house, BJ—our tiny cocker spaniel—came charging around the corner and leapt up at Larry, playfully yipping the whole time. But it wasn't playful to Larry. Larry wasn't laughing. He was screaming.

"*Get it off me!*" he shrieked. "*Mommy GET IT OFF!!!*" Then Larry bolted, dashing from his mother and disappearing into our house. A moment later, I heard the bathroom door slam. BJ, meanwhile, thought this was part of the fun and was still leaping up and down in our kitchen, still making those yipping sounds. I bent down to pick him up, feeling a lot like Dorothy in *The Wizard of Oz*, picking up Toto and trying to explain herself to that awful witchy neighbor.

"BJ didn't mean to hurt him. Honest, he's a really nice puppy."

Mrs. Brahms leaned down and tousled my hair. "It's not your puppy, Dennis. Larry has a fear of dogs. We just didn't know you had one, that's all."

"Why would anyone be afraid of dogs?" I asked. "They're friendly, most of them."

A troubled look came over Mrs. Brahms' face right then, one I didn't really understand until later. "He was attacked as a baby," she said. "He was playing in the dirt and this giant Doberman broke free from his leash somehow and just mauled him. Dug its teeth into Larry's arm. He still has the scars."

My mother gasped. "Oh my God. Was the dog rabid?"

"No, thank heaven," Mrs. Brahms said, looking up from me. "But it seems to have severely traumatized him. What he has is called *cynophobia*. He's been... well, we've been taking him to a therapist, a Dr. Stoker."

"Has it done any good?" Mom asked, glancing toward the bathroom.

"Some, yes," Mrs. Brahms was saying, but even at seven I could tell she wasn't convinced. "His doctor thinks it might be time to try exposure therapy." She sighed, looking down at my dog. "Although I'm not sure that's such a good idea."

Eventually, his mom coaxed Larry out of the bathroom, where he was crying in big, hitching sobs. BJ had been safely locked away in my parents' bedroom. The moment he walked out and looked in my eyes, I knew that I was going to be the one that had to protect him. In a way, that made me feel proud.

Except I didn't do so well. No, not so well at all.

* * *

We grew up together, Larry and I, and true to my thought that muggy summer day, I tried to protect him as best I could. The external stuff was easy; I filled out, got bigger, and played sports. I could make sure none of the inevitable bullies pounded on Larry, and that he always had a place to sit in the lunchroom.

But there was nothing I could do about what was going on inside him. At first, it was so subtle it was hard to notice. Little things, on the edges of conversation. He didn't like wearing watches. He wouldn't walk past a cemetery. Moths freaked him out. Like I said, little things, things bordering on sane. What I failed to figure out until much too late was that the things Larry didn't like were things he was *afraid* of. He didn't wear a watch because he was *chronomentrophobic.* Cemeteries bothered him because he was *coimetrophobic.* Moths—one of the big ones, as it later turned out—was his *mottephobia* exhibiting himself.

Larry collected phobias like other kids collected baseball cards. They seemed a source of perverse pride for him. Every time I would head on over to his house, he had new phobias to share with me, new levels of weirdness to delve into.

"Larry," I tried telling him one day after school, "this phobia stuff... it's not healthy. I mean, you know that, right?"

He was lying on his bed (which had no sheets on it by this point; he was too afraid of getting tangled up in them) and he sighed. "Dennis, do you think I *want* this? Do you think this is how I want to be?"

I decided to go with honesty. "Actually, Larry, yeah. It certainly seems that way."

He closed his eyes. "I know it sounds weird, Dennis, but I don't think it's me. It feels less like I'm *afraid* and more that I'm literally *made* of fear. Like it was here first and I was built around it. All it wants to do is get out. Does that make any sense?"

It didn't, and he was freaking me out too much for me to even begin to understand him. "You know, Larry, you have the power to keep it in. To not let it control you."

He laughed a little bit. "Dennis, you know as well as I do that I've never had that kind of control. This fear in me... I'm afraid." He laughed again, but it had no humor in it. "I'm *afraid* that it's not going to just be a part of me for much longer. I'm afraid that it will *become* me."

* * *

By our junior year of high school, Larry and I had begun seeing less and less of one another. Football was forefront on my mind by that point; I was beginning to decide that sports were my best way into college. When I wasn't training or playing, girls were becoming a priority. Besides, there had begun to be other friends, *saner* friends, and I had a feeling I was going to finish the rest of my high school days pretty popular. I guess that meant something to me then.

But I didn't let Larry completely fade out of my life, I need you to know what. That sense of duty kept bringing me back to his house at least once a week or so. I told myself that my presence in his life, how-ever limited, was going to keep him stable, grounded. I wonder now if I ever believed that lie, or if I just want-ed to. Because Larry wasn't staying grounded. Larry wasn't staying stable. Larry was getting worse.

One day, I picked him up in my car—which was already a challenge because he was afraid of the vinyl on the seats, the exhaust fumes, and the actual action of sitting—and told him that we were going out for do-nuts. "You like donuts, don't you, Larry?" I asked, my false cheer grating even on me.

Larry just turned to me slowly and said, "I can't eat donuts, Dennis."

"Why not?" I almost shouted, that false cheer fall-ing away. "What's wrong with donuts?"

"Dough mites," he said. "All through them. They don't die when they're cooked. They're in the food. You can't eat them, they'll kill you from the inside out."

"Larry, what's killing you from the inside out is not eating. You're going to die."

"No I won't," he said, almost crying. "No, my fear's going to keep me alive. My goddamned fear."

I couldn't take it anymore. I pulled my car over to the side of the road and told him to get out. He just looked at me with those pathetic eyes of his. "I'm sorry, Dennis. I'm so sorry."

"Get out, Larry. I don't need you and I don't need your fear."

He did and I drove away, trying not to look at him in the rearview mirror. When I did take a glance back, he was walking with his head down back toward his house. Whenever he passed a tree, he swerved away from it, as if it was going to reach out and grab him. That one was *dendrophobia*. The fact that I knew that just made me angrier, and I pressed my foot down on the gas and sped away.

* * *

I felt pretty righteous in my rage until I got home. Then the feeling miserable started. I picked up the phone to call Larry, but immediately slammed it down. He wouldn't be home for at least twenty more minutes, more if he was still contending with his fear of crossing the street. I paced around my living room for a while and suddenly an idea hit me. I went right to the phone book and went to the section marked **Therapists**. Two pages in, I found Larry's doctor, and called him at once.

To my surprise, he was actually in the office—I'd expected to leave a message. "Hello?" the man said, sounding unsure. "My secretary gave me your name but I don't recognize it."

"Dennis," I told him. "Dennis Harker. I'm a friend of one of your patients."

"Larry Brahms," Stoker said. "Yes, I know your name now."

"Dr. Stoker, I need to talk with you about Larry. I'm getting worried about him. Well, more worried. He's... he's getting worse."

There was a long pause on the other end. Then Stoker said, "I haven't seen Larry Brahms in almost six months," he said. "I wouldn't know what to tell you. And besides, anything I *could* say would violate the doctor-patient relationship. Dennis, I'm sorry, but..."

"Dr. Stoker, *please*. Larry's gotten... I don't know if this is the right term for it, but he's gotten *crazy*. And if I don't know how to help him, I'm afraid that he might do something really... maybe dangerous, or something."

"You're afraid?" Dr. Stoker asked.

I smiled a little, seeing the bitter humor in it. "Yeah. I am."

Another long pause, after which Stoker said, "Okay, Dennis. I'll meet you. There's a coffee shop on Columbus Avenue. You know it?"

"Espresso Express, yeah."

"Okay. Meet me there in one hour."

"Thank you so much! Thank..."

"Dennis? You said you wanted to know how to help Larry. I'm not sure I can tell you that."

"Why not?"

"Because, Dennis. I last saw Larry six months ago, and I came to the very rare conclusion... that he was beyond help."

* * *

By virtue of its proximity to the local college, The Espresso Express was crammed with students who had either partied or studied too hard the night before, and were now mainlining caffeine in a vain attempt to stay awake. *That'll be me in a couple years*, I thought with a grin. Then Larry floated into my mind and I realized it probably wouldn't be him in a couple years. This was normal. He was not.

I spotted Dr. Stoker at once; it wasn't hard, as he was the only person there over twenty-five. He sat in a booth in the corner with a steaming mug in his hand and a distant expression on his face. Settling in across from him, I verified it. "Dr. Stoker?"

"I used to want to be a teacher," he said. "Maybe that's why I come here. They never get any older, these kids. But I do."

"Dr. Stoker, about Larry..."

"Paranoid multiphobic," he said, taking a sip from his coffee. "Sounds almost musical, doesn't it? Sounds easy, too. Psychology is a wonderful field of study, Dennis, but it also has the tendency to pigeonhole. We do like to determine things, give things names and classifications. I gave that classification to Brahms almost a year ago. It's terrific to be confident."

"But that didn't last."

"No. Larry became... well, more erratic. More far-reaching." Stoker hesitated. "I could have my license revoked for even being here. This isn't right. I shouldn't be telling you anything that was told to me in confidence."

He moved to get up. I asked, "Did he ever mention dough mites?" For a long moment, he just sat there, paused, then slowly sat down again.

"No, never those. But he did say once that he couldn't go to the movies with you because of something he called 'dust voles' in the projector light."

I stared at him. "He said he couldn't go because of the dark and the vinyl on the seats. And the smell of popcorn, a specific osmophobia. He..." Then I caught Stoker's look and almost laughed. "And I'm mad at him for telling me one phobia instead of the other. It all boils down to crazy, right?"

"Not necessarily," Stoker said. "The dark, the vinyl, even the osmophobia... those are all real things. Concrete things. It's the invented phobias that began to worry me."

"Like the dough mites."

"And the dust voles. And liquid termites."

"You're kidding me."

"No. He was afraid to drink any water I offered him, lest the liquid termites infest him and kill him from the inside out."

"Liquid termites, Jesus. That's pretty much what he said about the dough mites, too. I was thinking about that on the way over, too, wondering if they might not be a symbol for something."

"Like disease, perhaps. Panthophobia?"

"Yeah, or even eating or drinking. Cibophobia or dipsophobia."

Stoker smiled. "It seems we're both an expert on phobias."

"You don't live this long with Larry without becoming one." I looked out the window. "But the symbol thing... it doesn't make any sense. Not for Larry. He wasn't afraid of going near windows because he was afraid of looking outside, you know? He was afraid of the glass itself. His phobias have always been specific."

"So this leads you to the conclusion that he really believes in dough mites and liquid termites."

"And dust voles, yeah. These are all real to him."

Stoker said, "They do fall under a category, though, these three 'invented phobias.' All of them deal with infestation. Brahms is afraid that these unseen creatures will somehow enter his body and eat him from the inside out." He paused. "And those aren't the only ones."

I looked at him, startled. "What do you mean?"

"Has he ever mentioned helminthophobia to you?" Slowly, I shook my head. I couldn't recall anything like that. Stoker said, "It's fear of being infested by worms. Most commonly, it's inexplicably linked to a fear of death or burial. But..."

"But not for Larry. He's got his own separate phobias for death and burial. This... *helminthophobia*... this is Larry actually being afraid of being infested by worms. Why?"

"I don't know," Stoker told me. "It's frustrating sometimes to not have the answers. I bring this up only because it was the last thing Larry mentioned before he stopped seeing me. And he did it under hypnosis."

"Hypnosis? Really? I thought that was fake stuff that magicians use. Sleight of hand type stuff."

Stoker shook his head. "No, Dennis. Hypnosis is a real, quite misunderstood science. What I was trying to do was to regress Larry, get him to get to the source of his dependence on his phobias. For a long while, he lay there, not saying anything. Then, very slowly, he said, 'Helminthos, Dr. Stoker. The worms, the worms, always the worms. Helminthos.' Then he snapped awake and ran out. I haven't seen him since."

"That's really creepy, isn't it?" Stoker hesitated, then nodded. "So what do we do now?"

"As I said on the phone, Dennis, I'm not sure it's possible to do anything. I came here today to give you some understanding, some background into the mind-set of your friend. As a professional, I am taught to believe that no one is beyond reaching. Serial killers, mass murderers, the criminally insane. All of them can be helped, can be treated, at least to a degree. But Larry Brahms... has shaken my belief in that credo. I'm not sure what to believe anymore."

"Me either," I said. Soon after, Stoker got up and left. I just sat there as day bled into night, and wondered if he was right. What could possibly be done about my friend?

* * *

I was still thinking about that question three nights later when the phone rang. My dad popped his head into my room, where I was lying on the bed, staring up at the ceiling.

"Hey sport," he said. "It's your friend's mother on the phone. Says he wants to see you."

I looked up. "Larry's Mom?"

Dad nodded, handing the phone out to me. I took it from him and said hello to Mrs. Brahms. "Oh, Dennis!" she shouted. "Oh, Dennis, it's wonderful. Larry! He's cured!"

My eyes went wide. "Cured? What do you mean cured?"

"He wants to see you Dennis! He's in his room and he wants to see you!"

I hung up the phone and grabbed my jacket. My dad stopped me as I was heading out the door. "Dennis? Be careful."

I looked at him. "It's just Larry, Dad. Don't worry."

"Every time you're with that boy, I worry, son. He's dangerous, you know."

"No, not dangerous," I said, hesitantly. "A little weird, maybe but... I'll be okay."

Then I was outside in the cool November air, and I had a lot of trouble believing myself.

* * *

I decided to walk over, wanting to clear my head before I met Larry. Cured? What did his mother mean, cured? Surely she didn't believe that he could have just gotten better overnight, could she?

I rang the bell at Larry's house and when his mother answered the door, she was smiling. Except for her eyes. Her eyes knew the truth, no matter how hard she was trying to believe otherwise. "He's in his bedroom, Dennis!" she said, excitedly. Now, in person, I could hear the panic edging into her voice. "He wants to see you!"

I made my way toward Larry's bedroom, knocking on the door once before I opened it. The room was dark, which startled me. Larry's fear of the dark had been legendary.

He was sitting on the bed, wearing a black hooded sweatshirt. The fear of the color black: melanophobia. One of Larry's most prominent phobias. Not, it seemed, anymore.

"Larry," I said simply, but I didn't know how to continue. He swiveled his head to look at me.

"Hey Dennis," he said, but he didn't sound like Larry at all. "Nice of you to drop by. I have some interesting things to show you."

"Larry, your mom said that you were cured. What did she mean?"

Larry reached down and grabbed a backpack from the floor between his feet. I noticed that the backpack was vinyl. Fear crept into me like a threat. Larry reached into the bag and pulled out a thick, battered book whose cover was just barely hanging on. I could read the title in the swatch of moonlight coming through Larry's bedroom window. *The Encyclopedia of Fears and Phobias*, it read.

"This has been my guidebook," he said. "Every time I get a new one, I check it off in here. They've been useful to me, my phobias. My fears. They've helped me to hide."

"Hide what?" I asked, now beginning to be terrified. "What are you hiding, Larry?"

"Oh now," he said. "That would be telling. I'd much rather show you."

"Larry, what...?"

"Follow me, Dennis."

"Where?"

Now he laughed, a shrill, high, child's laugh that sent shards of glass through my bones. "You'll see," he said. Then he got off the bed and walked slowly out of his room. I had no choice but to follow. Scared as I was, I was also curious. And yes, I still thought, in my idealist's heart, that I could save my friend. I still thought that as we made our way outside and up toward the cemetery.

But I was younger then. I'm much older than that now.

* * *

The cemetery at night is never exactly cheery, but tonight it was especially creepy. The trees were shed of their leaves and they titled toward the moonlight like ancient skeletons worshipping a faraway god. Ground fog crept around our feet in wispy, ghostly trails, cold and intangible.

"Larry, what is it you wanted to show me? Come on, show me so we can get out of here."

He stopped by a gravestone marked **Seward** and leaned against it. "All my life, I've been afraid," he said, taking off the backpack and holding it in front of him. "I've ruminated, Dennis, on the nature of that fear. Where it comes from, why it was so necessary for me to hold onto it. Whether my phobias were a part of me, or whether *I* was a part of *them*."

"Larry, you're scaring me."

"Now you know how it feels to be me," he said, dismissively. "About a year ago, I figured it out. I didn't come by fear accidentally. It found me. Possessed me. Made me its own."

"Larry, for God's sake…"

"Have you ever heard of helminthophobia?" he asked me, now reaching into his backpack again.

"It's the fear," I said, "of being infested by worms. Yeah, I've heard of it."

"I guess I shouldn't be surprised," he said. "Being around me all your life was bound to make you en expert." He laughed again, tittering like a lunatic. "I call it helminthos. It's me. It's all of me."

"I don't know what you mean, Larry." Panic had seeped into me, matching my terror. I wanted to run but I couldn't.

"Do you remember when I told you that all my fear ever wanted to do was get out?" From his backpack, Larry brought out a large butcher knife. Its blade gleamed in the moonlight. "I've been waiting my whole life, Dennis. Now it's time."

"Time for what? Oh my God, Larry, time for what?"

"Time to show you my fear," he said, and jabbed the knife into his wrist, sinking it in deep. Then he yanked it up toward the bend in his elbow, and blood spurted out across the blade. It looked almost black in the moonlight.

"Larry!" I screamed. "Larry, what the hell are you *doing!*"

But Larry wasn't listening to me. His eyes were closed and he was rocking back and forth. "They're coming!" he shrieked. "Oh, God, they're coming out!"

Then I saw them. Then I knew.

The spurting, black blood trickled off... and worms erupted from the gouges in Larry's arm. Hundreds of them, it seemed, then thousands, bursting from the screaming red slice in his skin. "My fear!" Larry shouted. "This is my fear!"

Worms roiled and squirmed under the flesh of Larry's other arm. He'd dropped the knife to the ground, but it didn't matter. They began to *burrow* out of his skin, writhing out, making holes bigger and wider before *pouring* out, flowing like water. Like blood. It dawned on me with fresh, clawing horror that the worms *were* his blood. The worms—his *fear*, they were his living *fear!*—were the only things keeping him alive.

They squirmed out of his chest, plopping down in tangled clumps to the cemetery ground below. They crawled out of his ears and his nose, creeping out of the corners of his eyes moments before the eyes deflated into flat, blind membranes and his sockets filled with worms. He opened his mouth to speak again and the worms issued forth, vomiting out like a poisonous meal that the stomach has refused. And they kept coming. They just kept coming.

"God," I whispered, and now I really was going to turn around and run. Tears streamed down my face. Blood pulsed blackly in my throat and temples. I squeaked it again—"God"—and before I could run, Larry's head exploded. Shrapnel of bone and flesh showered the graveyard, pale and sickly and grotesque. And I saw. God help me, I saw into Larry's skull. Where his brain should have been was a massive, squirming nest of worms.

Then I did run, pausing only to vomit by a tree on the way to my house. By the time I got home, I was crying hard, not only for my lost, scared friend... but for myself, as well.

You see, what Larry had said before he died began echoing through me, even then. Were his phobias a part of him, or was he a part of them? Put more plainly, what came first, the boy or the fear?

I lay in bed at nights, wondering just that. Wondering, and trying to listen for anything alien rustling beneath my own skin. Because if I've learned anything, it's that fear is transmutable, and that last night with Larry haunts my nightmares more and more each time I close my eyes.

What came first, the fear or the worms? I ask myself that every night, and I never get an answer. All I want is an answer.

Because I'm so afraid now. I'm so very afraid.

Baby, It's Cold Outside

The girl burst into Tapper's Tavern fifteen minutes past eleven on Christmas Eve. She wore a blue high school jacket with white piping, and a matching cheerleader's skirt. There was snow in her hair and her pale face was accented by heavy circles of red chapping her cheeks. Everyone turned to look at the girl as she pushed through the door, sending small drifts of snow scattering across the hard wood floor of the Tavern. The folks inside Tapper's looked at first out of curiosity, but they held their gaze long after that. What they stared at wasn't the girl's jacket—which weren't the colors of either of Falderdam's two high schools—or her ridiculously short skirt on such a blizzardy day as this. No, they stared at her because of the wide, protruding belly poking the jacket out in front of her like a giant, nearly-ripe pear. They stared at the girl because she was obviously very pregnant.

"Miss?" Darlene McLaren called from behind the counter. Herb, her husband, futzed with the radio dial some more. Only snippets were coming through now. The storm was picking up, it seemed.

The girl turned to her and locked eyes. The girl looked terrified. Her eyes reminded Darlene McLaren of a friend of hers from college named Rosa Greer. Rosa had gotten married early, and her new husband liked to beat her if the meals were cold when he got home from his job at the rendering plant, or if another guy looked at her on the street, or if he felt like it. Rosa's eyes had developed a scared, desperate look but Rosa herself had been powerless to get away. This pretty blonde girl with the high cheekbones and red cheeks had that same look in her eyes.

"Miss?" she repeated again. "Can we help you?"

"Damn thing," Herb said, smacking the front of the dial. A momentary burst of louder static came through, returning to its normal low buzz almost instantly.

"Don't swear, Herb," Darlene said on reflex, going over to the girl. She still hadn't said anything, only stared and shivered by the wall. Darlene looked past the girl into the restaurant area. Soozie Malone looked up from her mug of gin with drunken, hollow eyes. No help there. Harlan Blair, an old coot in his late sixties, sat with his head on his table, snoring away in the corner. A whole lot more no help. She turned back to Herb, whose entire attention span was taken up with fixing the goddamn radio. Even if she could get him to notice the girl, she wouldn't be able to drag him out from behind the bar. Damn. Doing everything herself, as always. A woman's work is never done.

"Are you all right, miss?"

The girl, who looked impossibly young to be carrying around what she was carrying, shook her head but did not open her mouth.

Is she mute? Darlene thought, her heart jumping at the idea. Soozie Malone and Harlan Blair, Falderdam's resident drunks, were one thing, but she quailed at the thought of having to look after a mute pregnant girl, as well.

Don't look like you got much of a choice, does it Darlene? she asked herself, the voice of her Ma clear as day in the front of her mind. She smiled a little. No, it don't.

"Miss?" she asked again, putting her hands on the girl's shoulders. At once, she could feel the girl's skin through the fabric. It was ice. "Oh, God," Darlene whispered, yanking her hands away.

"Cold," the girl moaned, her eyes rolling up to look at Darlene. "So cold."

Darlene craned her neck back to her husband. "Herb!" He continued to spin the radio dials, but she knew he'd heard her. After twenty-three years of marriage, she thought she knew the old coot pretty well. "*Herb!*" He looked up, seeming dazed and not entirely awake. It was his fallback, the pitiable face he put on so she wouldn't get mad at him for ignoring her. That might work with patrons at the bar who dismissed him as just an old fool. Not Darlene, though. She knew him better than that.

"Go on back to the storage room and get me a couple of them Army blankets." Herb grunted, but complied. Darlene turned back to the girl.

"Girl, what's your name?" she asked.

"Who izzit?" Soozie Malone called from the back of the restaurant. Her voice was slurred and thick.

"Never you mind, Soozie," she muttered. Then, to the girl, "Can you tell me what your name is?"

The girl looked up at her with muddy, wandering eyes. They seemed to float in her face like buoys on a dead sea. She opened her mouth and let a little puff of air out. "Too cold," she said earnestly, staring up at Darlene. "Him's won't come if it's too cold." Her voice came out in ragged segments, like a small child reading aloud from a complicated book.

Him? Who was 'him?' Something about the girl's words bothered her, but she couldn't put a finger on it.

"Is someone else coming, girl?" Darlene asked. No answer. Herb appeared at the bar with a couple of the scratchy wool blankets from the back closet, the words **Property of the U.S. Army** stenciled on the side. Darlene took the blankets and began to wrap the girl in them, looking her fingers and face over for signs of frostbite. She saw none. "Herb, help me get her sitting up in this booth." She motioned to the closest one, getting the girl under her shoulders.

"We ain't no charity, Mother," she heard him mutter as he got the girl's legs and hoisted.

Darlene looked up and glared at her husband. "And just what's that supposed to mean?" she asked.

"Means what it means," Herb answered calmly. Darlene began to feel her blood boil.

"Well, mister," she said to him, "Here's what I mean. This here's a pregnant girl, colder'n hell and in need of some help. It's Christmas Eve and I mean to help her. Now you can help me help her, Father, or you can sleep on the couch tonight."

Herb's mouth worked like a dishrag going through a ringer. The one sure sign that she had him where she wanted him.

Grudgingly, he said, "What do you want me to do?"

She smiled a little. "Try the police and the ambulance. See if there's any way they'll get this girl into a hospital tonight. I doubt it, though. If not, we'll keep her over tonight and get her there in the morning."

"Fine," Herb spat, turning and going toward the phone.

"Him's will be here," Darlene heard from behind her. The girl had grabbed the blanket around her and pulled it tight. Darlene looked at the heavy lump the girl's belly made in the wool and felt sad. How old must this girl be? Sixteen? Seventeen? It broke your heart.

"Who will, sweetie?" she asked. The girl stared ahead, not in Darlene's direction.

"Him's will come when it not cold," she said, "Him's won't hurt me anymore."

An alarm went off in Darlene's brain. "Hurt you? Who hurts you? Is it your boyfriend?"

The girl's eyes seemed to come alive at that. "Him's hurt me! Him's go inside me and hurt me!" Her eyes slowly returned to their sullied, nearly comatose stupor. "Only when it's cold. Only when I'm so cold."

Is she talking about being frigid? Darlene thought madly.

"What the hell's she babblin' about?" a new voice spoke up at Darlene's right. The sound startled her and she jumped a little. Soozie Malone stood there, her gin in one hand and her other gripping the coat hook fastened to the side of the booth.

"Jesus, Soozie," Darlene muttered, grabbing at her chest. "Darn near scared the daylights out of me."

"What about *her*?" Soozie asked in her drunkard's drawl. "She's givin' me the *creeps*."

"Just lay off it, Soozie," Darlene said, turning back to the girl. Her eyes had closed. Darlene reached out and wrapped her hand around the girl's. It was freezing.

"God*damn*," Darlene muttered. "Soozie, can you stay with the girl a second? I'm gonna go get the space heater."

"No-uh-uh!" Soozie barked, taking a step back. "I ain't getting' *near* that bitch." Darlene, who hadn't felt anything like flustered or out-of-control in years, stood up and faced the woman.

"How long you been comin' to Tapper's, Soozie Malone?" Darlene didn't give the woman enough time to puzzle it out. A heady stench of alcohol hung around her in a haze. She probably couldn't figure out two plus two right now. "Eleven years, that's right," Darlene answered herself. "And in all that time, I never put up a fuss about your bar tab. You comes in, you gets drunk, and you stays drunk. You pay when you can. There ain't never been a problem with that."

Soozie's eyes had gone dark and hot-tempered. She'd never been what one would call a mean drunk, but she'd never really had the opportunity to get into a mean situation. Now, maybe, the time had presented itself.

"And now yer sayin' there *is* a problem?"

"All I'm sayin', Sooz, is jus' watch the girl till I get back. It ain't a hard thing."

Soozie stared at Darlene with her hard eyes. Darlene stared right back. There was never any real contest, and both of them knew it. Soon, Soozie dropped her eyes. "I'll watch her. Just hurry up."

Without another word, Darlene moved from the restaurant area back to the bar. Herb was standing with his back to her, holding the phone to his ear.

"Hello?" He pressed the receiver button down twice: click-click. "Hello?" he asked with more urgency. Click-click.

"Nothing?" Darlene asked, putting a hand on his shoulder. He turned around, a scowl printed across his featured.

"No," he huffed, slamming the phone down on its cradle. "No signal at all, not even a busy signal."

"Phone lines must be down," Darlene said, taking an apprehensive look at the door. The wind outside whirled and whistled. If she were snug in her bed, next to her husband with three comforters on top of her, she would have smiled at the sound. Here, in the tavern with two drunks and a seemingly retarded pregnant girl, the sound was ominous.

"Wonder how long until the 'lectricity..." Herb began. Darlene put a finger over his lips.

"No, father, don't jinx it. Things is running fine now. They may just keep."

He smiled down at her. "Y'always were an optimist," he said.

"I'm too lazy to be th'other. Angry's hard work." She smiled again, then shuffled past him to the storage room.

* * *

"Everything hunky dory?" she asked Soozie, who had retrieved her gin and was now taking another swallow.

"Chick won't stop talkin'," she told Darlene, her voice slurring on the long vowels. Darlene looked down at the girl, whose eyes were now closed but whose mouth was moving faster than a puppy with his tail cut off. She moved her ear a little closer to the girl's lips.

Mixed in with what seemed to be babble, Darlene kept hearing "Him's comin," and "Gots to get warm," over and over like a chant.

"She crazy?" Soozie asked, looking as if she really cared about the answer.

"No, sh'ain't crazy," Darlene said, plugging in the heater and turning it on high. "She just cold, is all." But hearing those words repeat over and over from this cold, cold child—you started to wonder.

She started along that line of thought, when the door burst open again. Darlene jerked her head in that direction. A young man of about twenty-six stood in the doorway, wearing a bright yellow jacket and heavy gloves.

Is this "him?" Darlene wondered, not without some apprehension. "Hello?" she asked the man. "Hello, can I help you?"

The young man looked around at the faces staring at him. Herb, at the bar. Soozie, who was taking another swig of gin at a nearby table. And finally her, Darlene, with the nameless girl in a nameless booth.

"Are you open?" the man asked, sounding a little scared and a little lost. *But not crazy*, Darlene thought with some happiness.

"Yeah, come on in," she told him. He turned back, poked his head out the door and seemed to call to someone. His voice was carried away in the wind.

The man came back in, shaking the snow out of his hair.

"That's some storm," he said, smiling in the way people do when they're in new situations and aren't sure how to handle them. "Jeez."

Darlene looked down at the girl, who seemed to be asleep except for her constantly moving lips. Hell, maybe she talked in her sleep.

"The Blizzard of '78 was worse," Darlene said, smiling and sticking out her hand. The young man took it, seeming to be happy to be doing anything. "Darlene McLaren. You get lost?"

"Yeah," he said, shaking her hand and sounding a little sheepish. "Paul Ford. Me and my buddies were on our way up to Brown Bear Mountain. Skiing, you know?"

"Buddies?" Darlene asked, and as if on cue, two more young men came in from the cold. They wore the same loud jackets, one blue, one orange. *Rich kids from the city trying to brave the country weather*, Darlene thought. *Oh well, can't hold it against 'em.*

They introduced themselves. Loud Blue Jacket was Travis Cornwell, Loud Orange Jacket was Albert O'Connell. Cornwell was black, a fact that didn't go unnoticed by Soozie Malone, whose appetite for liquor was surpassed only by her appetite for men of the darker persuasion. Falderdam wasn't exactly rife with diversity, so on that front, at least, Soozie had been dry for a long spell. Now she removed herself from her booze (something Darlene had thought would need to be done surgically), stood and strutted over to where the boys in their ski jackets stood.

"Soozie," Darlene muttered under her breath.

"Well hey, sailor," Soozie said in a way that might have been cute were she a teenage girl. Her coquettish smile became a drunken leer on the face of a haggard, rapidly aging woman. She didn't seem to care, though, thrusting out her hand at Cornwell.

"Is it true what they say, dark man?" she breathed, biting a fingernail, a gesture which she undoubtedly intended as sexy, but what came across as a parody of lust. A bad parody.

"Um..." Cornwell began, looking confused and disoriented. He hadn't accepted Soozie's hand yet, and Darlene thought that was probably a good thing. Soozie just might eat it off.

"Knock it off, Soozie," she said, putting her hands on the back of Soozie's shoulders. Then, to Cornwell, "Don't mind her. She's a little... under the weather." Paul Ford smiled, brushing more snow from his jacket.

"Looks like we all are, ma'am," he said. Darlene returned his smile.

"Herb," she said. "Go on an' fire up the grill. These boys must be some hungry."

Herb grumbled, but that was just him. Darlene thought he'd be happy to have something to do other than complain about the phone not working and futzing with the radio.

The boys went to sit down when the third one—O'Connell—looked over and noticed the girl.

"Hi," he said pleasantly. The girl's eyes were half-lidded and she seemed to be drugged. She didn't respond. O'Connell said to Darlene, "She's not long, is she? She your daughter?"

"No," Darlene said, looking at the girl and shaking her head sadly. "We don't know where she came from."

"Is she okay?" Paul Ford asked from the table. "She seems a little out of it."

"I think—" Darlene began, but then the girl's eyes flew open wide and she started screaming.

"Him's hurt me! Cold and him's hurt oh so cold!" Then, as before, she abruptly stopped and went back to lying in her near-comatose stupor.

Darlene stared down at the girl for a moment. Then, she swiveled her head slowly to look at the boys sitting in their bright jackets at the table. Her eyes flicked back to the girl, the hideously pregnant child with the cheerleading jacket on, and Darlene wondered where she had come from.

The girl. Those boys. Something frighteningly maternal threatened to rise within her, but Darlene fought it back. Those feelings led to other, more distressing feelings. Panic, maybe. Rage. No, no, none of that would do right now. Christmas was a time for hospitality.

Still, as she rose from the girl to go help Herb with the grill, she couldn't help one glance over her shoulders at the boys. Big boys. Boys capable of doing things to a girl against her will.

No, she decided resolutely, and kept moving. She sensed it was going to be a long night indeed.

* * *

The boys ate quietly. Herb was back to playing with the radio dials. Soozie Malone was in a back booth, greedily eyeing Cornwell and nursing a glass of Scotch, neat. Harlan Blair was still asleep. Darlene scrubbed at the grill, taking all of this in with watchful eyes. Something in the air seemed ready to explode. At exactly 11:22 on Christmas Eve, something did.

"Mother, listen, I got something," Herb said, uncharacteristically excited. Carefully, he brought the radio over to Darlene and set it down on the counter next to the grill. The radio announcer's voice cut in and out maddeningly.

"...two school buses... football... *extreme caution...*" Then there was a high squawk of static, followed by nothing but white noise.

Darlene looked away from the radio. Her gaze settled on the three boys again, and then the mentally damaged pregnant girl in the booth next to them. *Extreme caution*: the words gonged in her head dully. It wasn't hard for her to fill in the blanks the radio had left.

School buses, full of children, slaughtered on the roadside. Absurd? Maybe. But they didn't exactly throw the words "extreme caution" when everything was hunky dory, did they?

All at once, she wanted to get that girl as far away from the boys' table as possible.

"Mother?" Herb asked.

"Shush up, Herb," Darlene said, distracted. As she watched, Cornwell stood up and headed toward the bathrooms. Like a lion stalking its prey, Soozie Malone stood and went after him. "You stupid woman," Darlene muttered, and left the area around the bar. Then, to Ford and O'Connell, she asked in an artificially cheery voice, "How are the burgers, boys?" Grunting, she settled the seat previously occupied by Cornwell and looked at the boys' earnest, smiling faces.

That killer, that Ted Bundy? He had an earnest face, too.

Another voice, the rational one that normally ruled her mind, countered, *That doesn't mean nothing, so you stop it!*

"Great, thank you," Paul Ford said, sopping up some spilled ketchup with the side of his burger. "Tell your husband these are the best burgers I've ever had."

Without changing her expression, Darlene said, "I'll be sure to tell him that." Then, smiling widely, "Say, you boys didn't happen to see anything strange on the way down here, did you?""

They stopped eating for a moment, considering. Ford began, "Not that I rem..." but O'Connell cut him off. "No, dude, remember? There was that deer? At least, I think it was a deer."

Ford's eyes brightened as his mouth turned down into a grimace. "Oh yeah! Jeez, that was sick."

"What was it?" Darlene asked, her curiosity forcing her to put all pretenses aside.

"Well, we think it was a deer," O'Connell said, "*Used* to be one, I mean *wow*. Guts everywhere. *Blood* everywhere. The damn thing was totally torn apart."

"That so?" Darlene asked, trying to picture the slaughtered deer in her mind. She kept side-stepping to the thought of slaughtered children, though. Two busloads of them.

"It was gross," Paul Ford was saying. "We found a set of antlers in the snowbank, like something ripped them off. I'd'a thought a wolf did it, or a bear, but I don't think there are wolves or bears in this area." He scooped up a French fry and popped it in his mouth. "I tell you, if I don't have nightmares about that thing, it'll be a miracle."

That was when the high, pleading shriek of a woman shattered the air, and the young pregnant girl in the cheerleading jacket began to cry out in unison.

* * *

Darlene looked around to where the screaming had come from in time to see Soozie Malone stagger out of the men's room, holding her face with one hand and her belt buckle with the other. She appeared to be crying. Her emotions now zigzagging everywhere, Darlene reluctantly stepped away from the screaming teenager and went to Soozie.

"Soozie, what happened?" she asked, keeping her raised voice stern and authoritative.

"That... *man*," she drawled, a combination of drunk-speak and crying. She pointed vaguely back to the bathrooms. "That *black* man! He was *tryin'* something with me!"

Darlene held Soozie out at arm's length and looked at her. There was a red mark on Soozie's face, the imprint of a hand. Her makeup was smeared, but that could have been her own tears. The most damning evidence of all was the front of Soozie's pants: her belt was askew and Darlene could just make out the top of her panties. They were ripped.

A moment later, Travis Cornwell burst from the bathroom, starting toward Soozie with anger in his eyes. Acting on instinct alone, Darlene grabbed Soozie away from the man and pulled her into her arms, stroking her hair. The pregnant girl stopped screaming abruptly, as if a switch inside her flipped off. She started sobbing quietly. Darlene cast her a troubled look, then turned back to Cornwell.

"What did she tell you?" he yelled out at Darlene, rage distorting his face. Darlene backed up more, wishing she was near the counter and the sharp kitchen implements. "What did she *tell you*?" Cornwell demanded, little specks of spit splattering Darlene's face.

Darlene moved Soozie behind her. *I will not be scared of this man*, she thought. Then, her mind conjured those two words the radio announcer had intoned: *extreme caution*. They seemed to float before her eyes in red horror-script. Two school buses. Extreme caution. And could she picture Mr. Travis Cornwell slaughtering his way through both of them? Yes. She could. But she didn't back down.

"She said you were *trying* something with her," Darlene barked angrily. She could have her own rage, yes she could.

"Mother..." Herb called out from the grill. Behind her, Soozie was moaning and muttering. From the tavern, the young cheerleader was still crying out her garbled, nonsense speech.

"Shut *up!*" she screamed, planting her hands over her ears. When she removed them, Tapper's was silent. Cornwell still stood in front of her, looking stunned but still angry.

"Listen, miss," Cornwell said, his voice more moderated now. "I don't know what that *woman* told you, but I didn't lay a hand on her."

"She's been slapped," Darlene said, her voice shaking minutely. The image of Cornwell slicing his way through a group of high school students still pervaded, but it had diminished a little. "Her pants are undone."

Cornwell's rage seemed to come back. "*She did it herself!* She came into the bathroom with me. I was taking a leak. She tried to, you know, *grab* me, and I told her to lay off. I'm not interested. Then she went all crazy, screaming and yelling, slapping herself 'cross the face, taking her pants down. She's crazy, you know that?"

Darlene let her gaze linger on Cornwell awhile longer. Then, she turned back to Soozie. "Is that true?" she asked. Soozie burst into tears, covering her face, but didn't answer.

Sighing, Darlene said to Cornwell, "Go back. Sit with your friends. Stay in sight." Cornwell seemed about to say more, then thought better of it, and went back to his friends. To Soozie, she said, "You, go sit down. Stay away from the boys. If you go near them, I'll kick you both out."

"Oh fine," Soozie said, wiping her face with the back of her hand. "Take his side."

"I ain't taking anyone's side," Darlene said, surveying the patrons of Tapper's Tavern. "I just want to keep peace."

After a moment of complete silence, the girl in the cheerleader outfit began to moan.

"Almost time," she said, and her voice had lost that hysterical, near-lunatic quality. Now, she sounded as drunk and slow as Soozie Malone on any given night. Darlene went to the girl and knelt down in front of the booth, holding the girl's hand. Beads of sweat coalesced in the hollow of the girl's palm. She was warming up.

"Almost time," the girl repeated, slower still. "Almost warm now, almost warm enough, almost time, baby."

Paul Ford turned to look at the girl. He asked Darlene, "Is she gonna give birth?"

Darlene put her hand on the girl's forehead. Under her breath, she muttered, "I don't know. I hope not. We are ill-equipped here. Father, keep trying the phone." Herb nodded grimly and went to it. Darlene stood and surveyed her tavern. The three skiing boys sat around the table, at the center of everything, not speaking. She let her eyes settle on Travis Cornwell, and that scary part of her mind opened up again, the part that allowed her to imagine Cornwell hacking his way through two busloads of children. Then, that part opened wider and she added Al O'Connell and Paul Ford to the fantasy. Even more gruesome. Her eyes flicked over to Soozie, and her brain automatically placed Soozie in one of those buses. Darlene permitted a small grin to touch her lips. Even drunk, sleeping Harlan Blair over in the corner could be the one. That's what her mind was telling her, wasn't it? *Extreme caution*, and that could mean anything had happened. Anything at all.

Her eyes turned to the girl in the cheerleading outfit, and for the first time wondered why any school would let someone as pregnant as she was continue cheerleading. The question gnawed at her, as if there was something important about the girl, something she should know, but couldn't quite grasp.

Before she could follow that train of thought, Herb interrupted her with a touch on the shoulder. "Mother," he said, "Phone's still out."

"Well there's a surprise," she said, not surprised in the least. "Herb, you keep an eye on the troops. I think I'm gonna go visit the lav."

Wearily, she made her way to the restroom near the back. She closed the door and locked it behind her, sighing heavily. Out of the corner of her eye, she could see the side of her face in the paint-spattered mirror over the sink. It didn't look good. Darlene McLaren was an old woman. She faced herself, a woman who has given too much and received too little. Kids who ran away from Falderdam as soon as they were old enough. Cold winters that settle into your bones and don't leave until long after the spring thaw. And this place, Tapper's Tavern. For twenty years, she'd owned it, and for twenty years she never showed much of a profit. What kind of life was that?

"No life at all," she told her reflection, and that was when the lights went out.

* * *

"Darlene!" Herb yelled from the bar. Darlene flung the lock open and fled into the front. The emergency lights connected to the generator out back glowed fiery red in the otherwise complete blackness. Paul Ford was standing up, a confused, frightened look on his face. Darlene didn't blame him. While Darlene was out of the room, Soozie Malone had taken the opportunity to rush up to the bar. Instead of helping herself to beer or Scotch or anything else, Soozie had helped herself to Herb's shotgun. She had it pointed at the table where the boys were sitting.

"Teach you," Soozie said in a drunken slur. "Look at me!" she screamed, grabbing at the front of her shirt. "I'm a *woman!* Can't you *see* that?"

"Soozie?" Darlene said, her heart pounding in her chest. "Sooz? Put the gun down, okay?"

"No!" she yelled out, sounding a little like the retarded girl—

Would they let a retarded girl be a cheerleader?

—who was moaning in the booth near the boys. Soozie swiveled her head toward Darlene, keeping the gun trained on the boys.

"He's a *man!*" Soozie wailed. "Can't he see I'm a *woman?* I ain't had a man in so damn long!"

"Soozie," Darlene said slowly, advancing.

"Don't you come any closer, bitch," Soozie said. "I'll plug you one, you best believe it."

"Soozie, you're drunk," Darlene said, thinking it was the understatement of the year. "You don't want to do this."

The woman's voice was choked up with tears. "All the men," she said in a softer voice. "They all laugh at me, I know they do. And they call me Soozie the Boozie and they go on home and they never take me with 'em anymore. I used to be pretty, you know."

Darlene moved a little closer. "I know, Sooz," she said, trying on a smile. "You're... you're still pretty."

"Then why," Soozie heaved, "Did he say *no*?" Her eyes had closed down to slits. Darlene flashed a look at Herb, who was standing behind Soozie to the left. Herb caught her glance, and Darlene motioned her head slightly. *Grab her*, the motion said. Herb offered a slight nod, then trained his sight on Soozie.

"No more," Soozie was saying in a low, dark voice. "No more men saying no to Soozie Malone." She raised the gun and aimed. Darlene saw that it was pointed right at Travis Cornwell, whose hands were in the air and whose eyes were wide.

"Now!" Darlene yelled, and several things happened at once. Herb leapt at Soozie, colliding with her and pushing her to the side. The gun went off, and the brilliant spark from the end of the gun illuminated the Tavern for a moment. Paul Ford suddenly started screaming, his bright yellow ski jacket now splattered with red. And off to the side, in her own little booth, the pregnant girl in the cheerleading outfit began to shriek.

"HIM'S COMING! HIM'S COMING NOW!"

* * *

Darlene's eyes went wide. Al O'Connell and Travis Cornwell leapt to their feet, staring down at Paul Ford, who had collapsed to his knees by the side of the table. Soozie Malone clutched at one of the barstools behind her, and she swayed back and forth as if her legs were full of water. She had dropped the shotgun to the floor, and Herb had picked it up. He now held it limply at his side. Through it all, the teenage girl continued to scream.

Feeling her mind would snap with panic if she didn't make some type of decision *right now*, Darlene rushed over to the girl in the first booth. In the emergency lights, the sweat coalescing on the girl's face looked like liquid fire, burning down her cheeks and streaming from her forehead. Abruptly, the girl's piercing screams ended, replaced by thick, guttural grunting.

She's pushing it out, Darlene thought wonderingly, that sense of panic flapping around her mind like a caged bird. *Him's coming*.

The girl staggered to her feet, fricative choking sounds hacking from her throat. Her head swung down, her limp blonde hair hanging in clumps, her mouth open lazily as if on a hinge. Darlene grabbed the girl's hand and almost pulled back. Heat baked from the girl's skin as if it were on fire.

"You gonna sick up, girl?" she asked, and as if in response, a large green-beige mass of vomit fell from the girl's mouth and spattered on the floor. Now sounds of whimpering and crying accompanied the girl's gagging noises. Darlene set her face and nodded. "You go right ahead, girl, it's all right."

"That bitch killed Paul!" Travis Cornwell was saying from far away. Even farther, Herb was yelling at Soozie to stay put. All Darlene's attention was on the girl.

"Him's," the girl whined, almost apologetically.

"Okay," Darlene said, not knowing what else to say. She wanted to get the girl to lie on the floor so the baby didn't fall from her standing up. But somehow, that didn't seem very important right now. An idea as distant as the sound of Herb's voice.

"Sorry," the girl moaned, and then issued a giant, hitching heave. She fell to the floor in a tangle, letting go of Darlene's hand. She heaved again, and an enormous spray of sputum shot from her mouth, splattering against the dead body of Paul Ford.

I'm gonna sick up myself, Darlene thought, but then all the voices in her mind ceased. The girl spasmed again, a convulsion that wracked her entire body. A thin rime of foam formed around her lips, her eyes bulging.

What is it? was the clearest thought running through Darlene's head when she saw it: some black liquid thing oozing out of the girl's mouth like tar. It flattened out into a puddle in front of the girl's face, a neat little circle of pure black nothing. Jutting from the center of it was a thin, curving column, twisting and writhing like a snake. The other end of the column seemed to grow from the girl's open mouth, somehow tethered to her insides through some obscene biology. Darlene looked at the still, black puddle and its black umbilicus and felt very cold.

"Mother?" Herb asked from the bar. Darlene's eyes flicked to him in panic. At once, the black puddle shot across the floor, elongating, stretching itself like a rubber band. The girl, whose eyes had closed tight against the horror playing out in the tavern's red lights, began to make thick, glottal sounds. The black thing stretched more. The girl screamed out. The end not connected to the girl—the puddle-end—flattened out again, its head making the shape of an ebony diamond. As Darlene watched, her horror mounting, the end of the thing separated, splitting in two like a double-headed snake.

"*Herb!*" she shouted, out of reflex rather than any rational thought. Herb didn't appear to hear her. Instead, he gaped at the snakelike thing slithering toward him. He didn't seem to remember he had the gun. The forked end of the black thing met with Herb's work boot and circled around his ankle tightly. The girl heaved another choking gasp, and the cord between she and Herb yanked itself back, jerking Herb off his feet and sending him crashing to the linoleum floor.

He dropped the gun and sent it scuttering across the tiles. Darlene shot a look at it, then back to Herb. The snake-thing had encircled his entire leg, wiry ropes of darkness like ivy creeping up toward his belly. Darlene tore her gaze away from Herb, fighting through the terror, and ran toward the shotgun. She bumped into Soozie Malone and knocked her over, sending her sprawling. Soozie didn't seem to mind, her mouth hanging silently open, her head craning up to watch what was happening to Herb.

"*Mother!*" he screamed, his leathery voice choked with dread. Darlene grabbed at the shotgun and lifted it, spinning around and aiming. The black wiry thing had circled Herb's entire body now, pinning his arms to his sides, and Darlene's only thought was that whatever that thing was, it was frighteningly fast.

She cocked the shotgun. In the dim red light, the gun metal glowed.

"Lady, no!" one of the boys—she didn't know which one—screamed out in the split second before she squeezed the trigger and the bullet found its mark. The girl, who had stumbled in a scant few hours ago wearing a too-short skirt and a cheerleading jacket, exploded in a violent ball of blood and bone. The sharp, acrid scent of gunpowder permeated the air.

Darlene exhaled shakily, unable to look at anything for a moment but the gaping crater she had made of the girl's stomach. Blood spurted from her in jets. She spasmed briefly, then stopped moving altogether.

Except for the part of her Darlene had tried to kill.

The writhing black thing seemed to caress Herb's cheek with one of its split tendrils. Herb screamed out. The snake-thing's two halves reconnected, seeming to flow back into each other like liquid, and as a whole, it thrust itself into Herb's open mouth.

"No!" Darlene screamed, then watched in sick horror as Herb's throat bulged and constricted. The tail-end of it slunk out of the girl's dead mouth and flapped to the floor, leaving a thin trail of the girl's blood behind. Darlene leapt forward, moving only on instinct, and grabbed at the tail. She caught it and yanked it back. An angry, powerful jolt of energy shot into her hand and reverberated up her arm, as if she'd jammed a set of tweezers into an outlet. In more surprise than pain, she limply released the tail end, and it disappeared into Herb's mouth.

The survivors—Darlene, Soozie, Travis Cornwell and Albert O'Connell, gathered around Herb's prostrate body, leaning over to look at him. The blood-soaked tail had made dark swatch-marks on Herb's white T-shirt. His chest moved up and down, but his eyes had glazed over. Darlene thought his eyes looked like the eyes of the dead.

"Him's warm now," she heard her husband say in that low, drunken speech. "Him's hungry."

Before Darlene could react, one end of the black, wiry thing shot out of Herb's mouth and settled in Soozie Malone's hair. Swiftly, it tangled itself in her dirty, mousy curls. Darlene heard a sound—unmistakably electric, like a small burst of lightning over a distant field—and then the black ropes began to sink into Soozie's skull. The smell of burning hair, then flesh, was nauseating. And below it all, below the stench and the horror, and the screaming behind her, Darlene could hear the sounds. The sucking sounds. And Herb's belly began to get fat.

In the second before she ran, Darlene thought of the buses full of schoolchildren. She wondered if one of the students—maybe even a driver—had carried this thing on board with them. She wondered how long it had taken this thing to devour two whole busloads of kids. How long would it take to devour the three of them standing here—and of course, Harlan Blair, who was still asleep in the corner. How long? Five minutes? Ten?

Without looking back, Darlene dropped the shotgun and ran screaming to the front door. It was cold outside. So cold. Him's couldn't survive in the cold, wasn't that right? Panicky, she reached the door, the high shrieks of pain behind her far off. Darlene McLaren flung the door open onto Christmas Day, and was about to thank the Lord for sparing her when something sticky closed around her ankle and pulled her back inside.

Funhouse Frank and His Zodiac Freaks

Now you have a problem, don't you, Alex? You mull these plans over, you think you have everything mapped out, but when it comes right down to it, you never quite think everything through. Now look. You've got a pair of dead Siamese twins here, a shitload of blood all over the desk where he (they?) was balancing the books. You've got the money, sport, but what are you going to do about the blood? Or the body?

"Shit," you grumble, shoving wads of the sticky greenbacks into your pockets. "Shit, I'll just take the money and run, like in that Eagles song." But what about Virgo, Alex? She complicates things, doesn't she? With this money you were going to run off to Mexico with her, and live the rest of your life on a beach by the Pacific. Fuck her whenever you can, because she never loses her cherry—finest snatch you've ever had, isn't that right? Every time like the first time—tight and smooth and bloody.

Speaking of bloody, buddy-boy, you've still got a mess to clean up here. Don't think too hard. It's all really simple. You grab Ted and Ed by his (their?—shit, Siamese twins are confusing) armpits, haul him out back behind the tent and get to digging. The grave will have to be a little bigger than the one you dug for that job in Jersey a few years back, because of the extra head and arm and leg, but you probably won't even break a sweat. Then, come back, swab up the blood, and you're on easy street. Tell everyone Ted and Ed must have run off with all the money—damn shame, really. Never trust twins, everyone knows that. And later on, you'll collect Virgo and get her into the truck, then head southeast until you hit the Mexico line. If she makes any trouble, it's no problem to pop her off when you cross the border, do the shallow grave dance for her by the side of the highway. Perfect.

Frank's emceeing the freak show down the end of the boardwalk—that ridiculous voice, always booming with ridiculous pride—which means you'll have about two hours to get everything cleaned up. You start to heft the body, when *she* walks in—your little Virgo, your little cherry. And then she starts screaming, and you can't listen to that shit now, and you can't let anyone else hear that shit either. You drop the body on the floor and run over to her, clamping a big, work-rough hand over her pretty mouth.

She looks at you with fear in her eyes—the blue glitter she painted on her temples shine in the light of the bare hanging bulb of the tent. The scared, helpless look in those young eyes—it turns you on, doesn't it? You want to see that look go deep when you take her and make her bleed again. You've already got a half-chub just thinking about it.

But now is not the time. Now is most definitely not the time.

"You gonna scream?" you ask her, whispering in that tough, gruff voice you usually don't use unless you're bopping her. Getting stiffer, there, buddy, don't lose your train of thought. She shakes her head, staring at you with those intense eyes.

"Good." You take your hand off of her mouth but still hold firm to her arm. You're no dummy.

"Alex," she begins, her voice squeaky like a little girl's. But how wrong was that, anyway? She's only nineteen as it is.

"Shut up, chicky baby. Why are you here, not at the show with Frank?"

"I forgot the arrows... f-for Saj."

"One of these days Saj is gonna take one of those arrows in his head and it won't heal up," you grumble, snickering. You see the pained, hurt look in her eyes when you talk about her brother like that, but it's good to have that look there. Easier to keep her in her place. "Okay, good," you say. "Here's the deal. You see we got a situation here—kinda bloody. I'm gonna clean this up and blame the whole thing on those two freaks." You point back at Ted and Ed, lying dead, a bullet through each head. You smile at that one—smart, Alex, very smart—and then go on. "I get the money, you and I split tonight, and no one will be the wiser until they find us gone."

"But Alex," she sighs, "You didn't have to *kill* them." She always pisses you off like this—whining and complaining. This is the way the world works, baby, you scream at her silently, better get used to it now.

"What did you think we were gonna do? Win the lottery? I told you I'd get the money and I did. Now what you do is get your arrows, go back to the freak show, and I'll meet you there when I'm done. I'll tell everyone I can't find Ted and Ed anywhere, or something." Again, that nagging realization that you never really get a plan together before you start acting on it. But no need to dwell. Introspection's for philosophers, right? You grab Virgo by her cheeks, squishing her face into a fish face—maybe she should have been Pisces, huh? "You don't tell no one, you hear me? *No one.*"

She nods. Wouldn't it be easy, so easy, to just off her, too? Right now, just come up behind her, make her fellate the pistol a little before you blow her brains out? But no. She's in the middle of the rehearsal, and Frank would come looking if she didn't come back immediately.

Lucky for you, honey, you think, and watch her as she gathers her arrows and leaves. Good—no more distraction. You've got everything under control.

Don't you?

* * *

The operation takes a little longer than you ex-
pected, and in the end, you actually do break a sweat.
You're running it a little close, there, aren't you Alex?
It had taken at least an hour to bury the body, and you
still have a lot of work to do, cleaning up the blood.
Better rush it up a little, wouldn't you say?

You find the sponges in the closet-sized bathroom,
and just as you're about to rush back in, you catch
a glimpse of yourself in the mirror. Haggard, grizzled
face, hanging down in doughy folds. Goddamn, how
did it ever get to be like this? You thought the carnival would be a fun, exciting life, didn't you? Now look
where your dream got you. Risking your life to grease
Ferris wheel joints at four in the morning, cooking for
a dozen sideshow freaks, and sometimes doing a little
murder or two on the side. What kind of life was that?
Not yours, no way, not anymore. With the money you
got from Ted and Ed, you can bring Virgo down to
Mexico, and live out there forever. Not a care in the
world. And if she ever presented a problem, wham,
bam, thank you ma'am—she didn't have to be a problem for long. Maybe you'd even have fun with it, poke
her in the crotch with a knife and see how many times
she can bleed fresh before she bleeds out. You grin
your dark little grin, and head back out to the count-
ing table.

You're about to start scrubbing when your eyes
catch something you've never quite noticed before.
Hanging on the wall behind the desk is a framed clip-
ping from some local paper. The headline reads: *Local Genetics Professor Lauded at National Convention.*
Below the headline, there's a picture. The glass over
it is grimy but the face is instantly recognizable. It's
Fabulous Frank, his ringleader duds swapped out for

a double-breasted suit and his top hat nowhere in evidence. "What the hell?" you mutter, wanting to read more... but now's not the time. You've got wetwork to do.

It takes time, but you have the energy. It's anger that fuels you, isn't it? Anger and horniness always give you that added strength, that focused precision to the task at hand. You wonder briefly—and without knowing it—why rage and sex always seem to go hand in hand with you. But that's a little too deep for you, isn't it Alex, and soon the thought is gone. So, finally, is the blood. Your work is done here—no one will know you've been here at all. Unless the numb cunt tells them, but she's so tight under your thumb she squeaks.

There's a mini-fridge next to the door and you drop into a crouch by it, hoping the twin fucks had a taste for Stroh's. Murder's thirsty work, especially when it's done double, and a beer would go down real smooth right about now. Then again, beggars can't be choosers. You'd take a fucking Moxie if that's all there is.

But the fridge is mostly empty, and you're about to slam the door when you notice something at the very back. You reach in and almost prick yourself on it; it's a syringe, filled with some opaque liquid. Is it Gemini's? You examine it for a moment then toss it back into the fridge. Gemini sure isn't going to miss whatever it is, but you have the feeling that someone else might. Safer to leave everything as is for now.

It's a perfect plan, pulled off perfectly. You're right proud of yourself, aren't you? Go ahead, man, pat yourself on the back. You didn't forget anything, did you?

Did you?

* * *

It's the end of the show, and Fabulous Frank seems to be having a great old time with his freaks on stage. You keep asking yourself why this crowd of people would pay money to see the Zodiac Freaks— you see them every day and they turn your stomach. Let one of these rich bitches or bastards with their seven figure incomes and their BMWs or Saabs clean up the blood after one of the "performances" for once. Or clean out the Port-A-Sans after one of the freaks take a leak—Aquarius always overflows the damn thing and you have to clean it up. Or watch them eat while they're cleaning the trailers; yeah, that's always fun. Leo pounces on the chickens you toss into his cage—live chickens, of course. Frank would have it no other way. Yeah, it must be fun to watch Leo tear the head off of a chicken for a night, but let any of those fuckers watch it day in and day out, chicken guts you have to clean up, and puke, and blood, and you just can't take it anymore, can you?

No. But now you've got the money—all the money, all the rich fuckers' summer spending money—and you're gonna make a break. All the way down to Mexico, you and Virgo, Merle Haggard on the radio and nothing but freedom.

On stage, the ringleader, Frank, stands off to the side to watch the final freak act. You've hated the guy since you first saw him—a tall, muscular man who always looked like he knew he was better than you, especially in that goddamned ringleader getup. Always talking about how the freaks are his family, how he's so proud of them. Never a good word for you, though, is there? You just serve and clean and take Frank's shit. No more. He's in for a rude awakening tomorrow, isn't he, when he finds out that the Siamese is dead and the virgin daughter skipped town with the janitor?

Speaking of Virgo, there she is on stage in her tight little sequined number. She pulls back the bow in her hands and launches the arrow at her shirtless brother, Sagittarius. His bearded, darkish face scrunches in a mask of pain as the arrow plunges into his shoulder. The audience gasps. You grin a little. You've seen this all before.

Saj reaches his left hand up and slowly begins to twist the arrow, grinding it, rending it from his shoulder. Blood and meat-gristle spatter to the floor as he begins to yank on it, harder, with more vehemence. Suddenly, the arrow comes free, and a brief freshet of blood issues forth. And then the miracle, what the BMW owners came to see. The large, meaty, gaping wound in Saj's shoulder begins to heal. The muscle retracts, the skin stitches itself from nowhere, regenerating almost instantaneously. In less than thirty seconds, the hole where the arrow was is no longer. Saj turns to the audience, pounds a heavy fist into his shoulder once, smiles, and bows. The audience claps uproariously. It's the show-stopper.

"Thank you, ladies and gentlemen!" Frank says, stepping out from the side of the stage and thrusting his arms in the air to encompass the entire room. "Thus concludes our fascinating tour... of the world of the Zodiac Freaks!" Applause. Every other word is punctuated by a further thrust of Frank's arms. You hate the fucker. He's too fucking happy. "I hope you enjoyed the show! Have a good night, and when you return, please... bring a friend!" More applause, and then they begin to file out. You rush up to the stage. Taurus and Aries, known in the show as the Horned Twins, are wheeling away the tank Pisces is sitting in, her odd, side-of-the-head eyes blinking under the tank's glow. You want to catch Virgo before she goes back, you want to set up the plan now. She's stupid, but she can remember to follow the rules. *Your* rules.

She's off to the side, talking with her brother. Saj looks up.

"Hello, *Alex.*" He spits your name, as if it were a cuss. You hate him. You hate all of them.

"Hey, Saj," you say, grinning. "Arm hurt?" Saj just shows his teeth, and Virgo tries to calm him. Ah, the pastoral family picture, except they're all fucking freaks. "C'mon, Virgo, we gotta talk."

"Now?" Dumb cunt.

"Yeah, now. Say bye to your brother and let's go get some burgers." She says her little goodbye, and you grab her arm and lead her down the stage stairs. You glance back once and see Saj glowering at you. It makes you feel powerful, in control, to have his little sister by your side. You don't really give a shit about her, except for the exceptional lay between her legs, but you really get off on the fact that it bothers Saj.

Don't you?

* * *

Most of the food booths are closed, but you just manage to grab a couple of corn dogs before Mabel shuts the fryolater down for the night. Working against the crowds, you lead Virgo into the shadow of the Wall of Death ride and lay it all down for her, real chilly. She'll meet you by the funhouse at two A.M., her traveling clothes packed. Easy as pumpkin pie. She nods in all the right places, and says, "Okay, Alex" every time she's supposed to. Maybe you won't kill her when you get to Mexico, after all. She's been well trained.

A cursory kiss on her little-girl mouth (she likes romance, the stupid bitch) and you turn toward your own trailer, dreading the return to the cramped hovel where you play King of the Cockroaches until you escape once more. Before you can leave, though, Virgo pipes up in that little-girl voice of hers, "They started asking about Gemini."

You stop, your face frozen in mixed fear and rage. Without turning back around, you ask slowly, "What did you say to them, babe?"

"That I didn't see them. That I was a little worried, because they hadn't had their shots yet today." The last word cracks, as if she said something she wasn't supposed to. What was this about shots? You wheel on her.

"What shots? I never heard about any shot." You raise your fist above her face, ready to strike if she says anything wrong.

"Th-they were diabetic, Alex!" she nearly screams, and you clamp a hand over her mouth again. Oh yeah, you perk *right* up at that.

You say, "Diabetic, huh?" as you release your hand. That explains the syringe in the refrigerator. She gasps a breath in.

"They took insulin shots. I usually gave it to them, before meals."

Looking into her pitifully pretty face, you mutter, "Oh, he got some shots today, all right." Then you giggle a little. Is that hysteria in there? No way. No, we're chilly up in here. You grab her face again and reiterate the salient points. "Two o'clock. Any later and I'll leave without you." You can't afford to take that risk—the risk of her knowing both that you killed Gemini and knowing the vague direction you would be going is too great—but she doesn't know that. It'll be much safer just to take her along, then decide what to do with her when you get across the border. Either way, killing or fucking, you'll still get off.

Won't you?

* * *

It starts to gnaw at you, though, the way Leo gnaws at his live chicken as it bleeds to death in front of the crowd. She could be blabbing the entire story to her "family" right now. It's midnight, two hours too early for the meeting, but the time feels right to jet. Sometimes you get those funny little twitches in the back of your mind, isn't that right? And usually, most of the time, those twitches have led you right. Away from the trouble in Jersey, before the heat got too hot. Out of the halfway house in Massachusetts, right before Bongo Benny, recovering crack addict, decided to take his knife to every sleeping throat in the place. So when the twitch twitches, you follow. Just like you're following now, your duffel bag slung over your shoulder and your pistol tucked safely into the front of your pants, out of the trailer and over to your pickup. Without knowing it, you're whistling "I Think I'm Gonna Live Forever." Screw the bitch—you need to get out, and get out *now*.

You throw your duffel bag in the back, and hear a sharp, frightened noise come from the cab. For a second, fear grips your heart and you start panicking. Then, a face pops up, and you see it's only Virgo, early for the meeting just like you.

"Alex? Is that you?"

"Shut the fuck *up*," you hiss, opening the cab door and glaring in at her. She looks scared—more scared than usual. It's not fear of you, not now. "What?" you ask.

"They found Gemini's body. I didn't tell them anything, I swear. Leo... he sniffed it out. They went around the back of Gem's trailer and found the pile of dirt. I ran. I had to hide. I wanted to get you but I didn't know if *they* got to you first. So I waited. I know a place to hide, something that none of the others know about."

Your head is whirling. They found the body? But how? Didn't you pat down the dirt well enough? Hide? What the hell...?

"Why not just take off?" you ask, your voice cracking in a panic that's not like you, Alex, not like you at
all.

"Because they called the police. They'll be here
soon, and they'll *find* us. But I have a hiding place
and we have to go *now*."

"You don't give the orders here, girly," you whisper, but it's just a reflex. When Virgo gets out of the
cab and starts off, you follow her. Past the shut down,
lifeless games booths. Past the monstrous, eerie Tilt-
a-Whirl, frozen in darkness. Past the Wall of Death,
past the Whip, past the hot dog stands, past the ticket
booths. All the way to the edge of the carnival, all the
way to the funhouse, its sides painted with scary-look-
ing ghosts and monsters. During the daytime, it looks
like a stupid little kiddie attraction. But not now, Alex.
No way. Now it's a *real* haunted house, just waiting to
eat up a scummy Jersey asshole like you, isn't it?

"No way, babe," you whisper, but your voice quiv-
ers. C'mon, man, you gonna turn pussy in front of
the chick? "Not in there." Good—a little stronger that
time.

"Alex, I don't think you understand," she begins,
and oh, how that voice is different, too. Not at all the
scared little-girl voice you usually hear out of her, is
it? Now, it's commanding, intelligent, and how the hell
could she have been hiding it all these months? "The
cops will be here any second. You've got almost a doz-
en freaks out for your head. You *killed* one of them,
Alex. Now, I want to get away as much as you do, but
I'm not going to go with you unless you *move*."

You're stunned. When did this mealy-mouthed little girl turn into a wise-ass little whore?

"Listen, babe..." you begin, unsteadily.

"We have time for your fucking power trip *later,*
Alex. *Now*."

You follow her into the funhouse, quietly, because
if you speak you will surely begin to scream. And then

you will surely begin to kill her, and we can't have that right now, can we? Not till you get to the cunt's little hiding place, where you can wrap your hands around her neck and choke the ever-loving life right out of her sassy little body. Two freaks are just the same as one. Then you can lay low and try to make it out in the morning. You've gotten out of worse situations before.

She leads you in the front door. It's supposed to be locked, but she has the key. She leads you in, and suddenly you are both plunged into utter darkness. Real fear grips your heart now—you hate funhouses—no clear direction of where you are going, no idea when or where some plastic ghoulie is going to pop out at you. Doesn't quite fit into your idea of Alex In Control, does it, buddy-boy?

"This way," she whispers, grabbing your shirt, and now contempt of her rises up to conquer your fear. She's going down, all right. You can't wait. But first, you need to get to get out of this utter darkness, to a place where you know the dimensions. You hate being disoriented, being out of control of the situation, being...

Suddenly, the lights come on, and Virgo's brother Sagittarius stands in front of you, grinning. You yank the gun from the front of your pants, point it directly at him, and fire. The bullet shoots straight through his chest, spurting blood; immediately, his body begins to heal itself. He rushes you as you continue shooting, catching his leg, his ear, even his throat. All the bullet wounds heal instantaneously, and as you shoot the pistol's final bullet, he grabs you, gets behind you, and puts you in a headlock. Now, he is able to wrench the pistol from your grip easily, tossing it away. He steps back, leaving you standing alone in the middle of the room. Without warning, something slams into you from the side, heavily, painfully. As you fall to the floor, you see Aries, a regular man but for the powerful, curled horns jutting out from his forehead. He struck you in the ribs, and you know that at least a few of them are broken. And you know something else, something you wouldn't have thought possible a few hours ago. You were led into a trap.

"C'mon, Virgo, Saj," Aries says in a gruff, angry voice. "Frank's waiting for him."

Virgo looks down at you, at the cracked, bleeding man lying on the floor of a large, open space in the funhouse. You see some plastic monsters on springs attached to the walls. Spooky fun for the kids, maybe. But this, this is real fear, my friend. Virgo bends down and spits in your face.

"Let's go."

The ram-man grabs you by the hair, and you shriek, the pain in your chest huge and screaming. You're being led down a corridor, dimly lit by the bare, spare bulbs above. And from somewhere—what the hell? Music, being piped in from some unknown place, drifting down into the dank corridor you're being led painfully down. You know the song almost immediately—whoever's playing it has a twisted sense of humor. It's Merle Haggard, of course, the last great country star. The song, slow, twangy, is "You Don't Have Very Far To Go."

Do you?

* * *

You are thrown into a larger room, even more dimly lit. You hit the floor on your side and you scream out in fresh agony. More ribs crunch inside your chest, and it's suddenly harder to breathe. Slowly you glance around. They're all here, all the freaks. Aquarius, who constantly leaks water from his pores, except in the show when he concentrates his will and *shoots* it out. Capricorn, "The Hoofed Wonder," shaggy hair hanging over his angry, goatish eyes. The Crab Woman, Cancer, three sets of sharp, cruel-looking pincers extending from her bald skull like Medusa strands. She is holding the boom box that is playing that song, that slow, soothing, dark song. All of them, all staring directly at you. And standing in the middle, of course, is Fabulous Frank.

"How nice of you to join us, Alex," Frank says, his voice dripping with dark humor. He smiles his dazzling white smile, the one the girls in the audience squeal about. Now, my man, it's your turn to squeal. "We are met under some unfortunate circumstances, I'm afraid. It seems you have killed one of my sons."

You say, "He wasn't your son." You try to be gruff, to manufacture that voice you used to use when you talk to Virgo. Now it comes out in a whisper.

"Oh, you wouldn't know, would you?" Frank says, chuckling. "Well, I suppose he wasn't technically my son—or sons. It's always a matter of semantics when it comes to conjoined twins, isn't it? Regardless, I'm the one who gave poor Gemini real life. But maybe I should explain.

"Before I came into this happy family, my life was dedicated to the study of human evolution. I was working on developing a gene..."

"You were a genetics professor," you say. Terror slips into you now, cold and hard and slithering.

Frank claps his hands together, his mouth wide in a grinning rictus. "*Very* good, Alex, give this man a *prize*! The function of my gene was to eradicate several steps of the evolutionary ladder at once, to bypass the millennia of struggle and hardships that species must endure to viably emerge. Imagine the ability to create entirely new species *at will*!"

Frank looks past you reverently, remembering. Under no will of your own, you mutter, "You're insane." His dazzling smile turns down into a frown, and he leers at you.

"That's just what *they* said. My colleagues, my *friends*. They all laughed at me. Called me a 'mad scientist.' Couldn't they see the possibilities? Couldn't they grasp the fundamental scientific worth of a *dual-species gene*?" He pauses, collecting himself. Terror washes over you in a wave. "No, they couldn't. Not at all. So they stopped my grant money, and eventually forced me out of the university. But before they did, I created, accidentally enough, something almost as effective as the inter-species gene. A formula." Frank bends down, staring you straight in the eye. "A *grafting* formula."

Your eyes widen. You can feel your bowels loosen. Frank stands up straight, extending his hand toward Taurus.

"Behold the bull! He used to be Richard Sematar, a petty thief from Lincoln, Nebraska. I offered him a chance to be rich and famous, if he was willing to participate in one of my first experiments. He was very willing, especially since I had his secret—a small little murder he had committed several years prior. And now you see before you Taurus! The Bull! A man with horns that actually grow from his head!" Frank yanks on one of Taurus' horns, and the man-bull grunts in slight pain. "You see, dear boy, my formula is revolutionary. It doesn't just glue parts of one being onto another. It regenerates tissue, skin, and bone matter, at the same time melding the two parts together. Richard's horns are actually a part of him now—he has actually become The Bull!"

"Same here, with Scorpio—those stingers didn't naturally come out of his forehead! I grafted them! Or Libra. Her scales used to be that of a Gila monster! Isn't it amazing?"

"You're sick," you say, staring at the freaks, staring at Frank. A thick, crawling horror writhes in your belly. You have never known fear this great.

Frank ignores you, and presses on. "But I didn't create all of them. Some were natural. Sagittarius, for one. Amazing ability to automatically regrow tissue.

The freak answer to my own genetic question. If I had known about him during my tenure at the university, perhaps I would have created the inter-species gene after all. And his sister, your little friend Virgo, she of the perpetual hymen. She comes in quite handy during the off-season. You wouldn't believe how much people will pay for even five minutes with a virgin! The only problem is, you can't have repeat customers."

You stare at Virgo, and she stands next to her brother, smiling with a dark, dark look you've never seen before.

"I wanted her to keep you around," Frank continues, "A willing pawn to my king. I thought you might prove useful. As it turns out, you have." Frank whispers something to Libra, who steps out of the shadows with something small and cylindrical in her scaly hands. It's a needle, and oh, you recognize it, don't you? You've seen it before. Viscous fluid floats around inside the clear glass, the color of sure death. Libra presses the plunger, squirting a shot of the liquid into the hazy air. "Gemini was a natural freak, as well, Alex," Frank says. "You have no idea how hard it is to find conjoined twins willing to be in a freak show. And you killed him. Them. Funny, those pronouns. But now, we need a replacement. And guess who just volunteered?"

Frank nods to Aries, who grabs you up from the floor and holds you in a full-nelson, so tight that you can only move your feet. Within seconds, Leo is below, holding even those steady. You can't move.

Out of the darkness behind Frank, Capricorn steps forward on hoofed feet. He is holding out a large pickling jar, but you can't quite see what's inside it. Frank takes the jar, opens it, and reaches inside.

"Say hello to your new brother, Alex," Frank says, then brings his hand out of the jar. He's clutching a dripping, half-formed human fetus by the top of its head, its tiny dead arms and legs dangling loosely in Frank's quivering fist.

Libra steps forward with the needle, and you begin to shriek, trying in vain to jerk your body away. She advances, pressing the point to your forehead, jabbing it in quickly several times, painfully, in a small circle. Your eyes look past her to Frank, who has produced a large pair of pruning shears, and is going about slicing one of the arms off of the fetus. Your screams intensify.

"Quickly, quickly," Frank mutters, as they bring the tiny arm closer to you, veins and a miniature knob of bone poking out from the sliced end. Suddenly, it is too much, far too much. The lights in the funhouse go dim, dark, and the sedated country rhythm of Merle Haggard follows you down. You find it's much more peaceful in the dark.

Don't you?

* * *

"Ladiiiiiieeeeees and gentlemen! Do I have a special treat for you tonight! *More grotesque* than the Bearded Lady! *More impressive* than the Strong Man! *More freakish* than any normal set of conjoined twins! I present to you... *Gemini*!"

The velvet cover over your head is lifted. Ropes bite cruelly into your arms and legs, and when you try to shake out of them, you find that the chair you're in is bolted to the floor. You try to say something, anything, but your mouth is duct-taped shut.

The freaks—The Zodiac Freaks—sit around you in a loose semi-circle. Frank stands behind them, smiling. "What do you think?" he asks, and one by one, they begin to clap. Why are they clapping? Why...?

Suddenly, a small, fleshy arm comes into your line of sight. You feel nerve endings tingle in your forehead, and you remember. Oh God, buddy boy, you remember everything.

Two small legs kick furiously from your chin. Looking down, you can see little toes twitching spastically. The fetus-hands protruding from your head reach down and rip the duct tape from your mouth. And as you finally are able to scream freely, you feel the staring half-alive fetus eye growing on your tongue blink, and your mind snaps.

Doesn't it?

Quarry Story

Poor guy, the girl thinks, dangling her feet down, *I guess he couldn't fly after all.*

1 / Now

Rachel McHugh glances briefly out the window and takes in the night, a small, sad sigh escaping from between her clenched teeth. Outside, the dark van sits like an ominous black monster, staring mutely down Kookaburra Lane. A sickle moon hangs above, throwing long shadows across empty streets and yards. It is nearly midnight, the witching hour, and all outside is silent.

The biggest shadow stretches out from her house, an expensive house her parents paid good money for. That oft-repeated phrase used to come a lot when she was young enough to draw on the walls with her crayons. "We paid good money for this house," her father would say, "Not just so you could destroy it." But recently, Rachel has discovered other ways of destroying the house, ways she is not proud of.

Again, she sighs, and looks back at the van. Her big, beautiful house seems to stand watch over the van, like a dignified schoolmarm would guard an unruly youngster, making sure he doesn't cause too much trouble. But tonight it is too late. The trouble has already begun, the cogs turning, and it has progressed to the point that stopping would mean ultimate destruction.

Rachel hears a voice calling from the other room; it is her boyfriend, Rip. She glances swiftly toward the door that separates the kitchen and the living room. Time to stop gazing outside and time to set the plan in motion. Looking back down at the pad of paper she has clutched it one shaking fist, she places it on the counter by the sink and begins writing furiously, calling for Rip to hold on a moment. Deep-sunset-red hair flows over her shoulders, picking up the impersonal shine of the kitchen fluorescents, transforming it into dark fire. She imagines her boyfriend, her Rip, sitting on the living room couch, sporting an almost painful hard-on. In her mind's eye, she can see his hair, almost the length of Rachel's, tied back with a string of rawhide, a fall of severe ebony. The television facing him vomits a blue-white glare, barely connecting with his hazed-over eyes. He is trying not to think of anything but getting it on with her. At least that's what she imagines. Maybe he feels some remorse. But she doubts it.

She puts down the pen, grabs two cans of Coke from the refrigerator, and enters the living room. Concentrating her efforts, she smiles a bit, then moves toward him.

The sodas aren't out of her hands before he grabs her. Kisses only of urgency, void of love or passion, fuse them; now there is just that animal heat to warm them. Rachel supposes she might like it a little, even now, even after everything. But maybe that was just pity. Pity, and a little longing for everything not to have turned out so wrong.

She breaks the kiss before he can lead her deeper, consuming her. In doing so, her mind flashes onto that first time with Rip. Her very first time, on the ledge of rock known as Streak's Revenge, down on the edge of town, in Tavin's Quarry.

2 / THEN

Rachel was aware in some vague way that she was bleeding, but it didn't hurt much and that was something. Rip's long black hair hung down in her face, oily and clumpy, but she didn't ask him to tie it back. It would take away from the moment.

But what moment? Looking up into his thin, mousy face, his eyes half-lidded, she knew she should be feeling something inside besides the somehow mechanical plowing below. Some of her friends (actually, they were more classmates than friends; she hadn't had any real friends since Erin Sanderson moved to Maryland two years ago) who had done it said it was awful—a lot of pain and a feeling of great loss inside. Some had told her that it was a type of magic, or elevation at least, to a place you couldn't even imagine. Rachel didn't feel either; all she felt were the sharp pebbles of Streak's Revenge poking into her back, the rhythmic in-out of Rip entering and exiting, and the gently lapping September air. No more, no less.

Streak's Revenge was a ledge jutting out midway down the wall of Tavin's Quarry, equally between the top, Hell Heights, and the bottom, Chicken's Paradise. It was the only ledge here large enough to accommodate their act, named by the local kids for a young boy named Freddy "Streak" Atchison from the Sheldon High track team. In 1982 Streak had jumped off into the deep Quarry waters, never to resurface. The officials never found a body, even after sending down skin divers and sonar devices. The revenge part came from the story the older kids told the younger kids: that Streak was plenty pissed off about having died, and now his ghost haunted the Quarry, seeking to exact the same fate as his upon unsuspecting jumpers.

But none of that mattered now, not to Rachel and certainly not to Rip. She lay, taken, on the middlemost ledge on this side of Tavin's Quarry, the stars and moon blocked out by Rip's dark tangles. Halfway between Hell and Paradise, and if she felt an emotion at all, it was an inexplicable sadness that seemed to wrap around the whole of her. Suddenly, everything was unsure.

3 / Now

She stops him before he can undo her pants buttons. Rip was frustrated enough when he saw she wasn't wearing one of her obscenely short skirts; now he's infuriated.

"What the hell's the matter with you?" he shouts petulantly. But Rachel hears something else in there, some scared tone, a frightened child inside the macho front. Could it be that Rip was as scared as she was? That he felt some shame? That he felt some remorse?

That she might be wrong?

But that was crazy talk, designed to cloud her mind and give her second thoughts.

Of course, that was a joke.

There was no turning back now.

"Nothing, Rip," she answers and smiles sweetly. If Rip were more perceptive or if Rachel were less guarded tonight, he might have sensed something in *her* voice betraying her words. But this was too important, too *necessary*, and Rip doesn't pick up on it.

"Nothing at all," she reiterates. "But my parents will be home early tonight, and besides, I want to go somewhere else."

"Where?" he barks, that other, smaller voice inside his regular one dissolving in a hopped-up ocean of hormones on hold.

"Tavin's Quarry," Rachel answers, a little seductively, and goes to get her coat as if he has already agreed. Rip mumbles something incoherent, then stands to join her.

Millions of thoughts buzz through her head, but she doesn't let any of them speak too long. She's committed to going through with this. These past few days—hell, these past few months—have been too much. Everything has gotten too far out of control, and everything has to stop sometime.

Rip has to stop tonight.

4 / THEN

"You're not going out there, Rachel!" Fran, Rachel's mother, called after her as Rachel made her way toward the front door. Tonight, she had rimmed her mouth in black lipstick, and had painted equally dark eye shadow on her eyelids. The effect of both against her normally pale skin gave Rachel the appearance of a walking corpse.

Glancing through the generous bay window overlooking the front lawn, Rachel saw Rip's black van poised there, ready to dart off. A momentary connection—that of a starved jungle cat ready to pounce on unsuspecting prey—crossed her mind, then vanished. She wasn't even aware the thought had been there.

"Leave me alone," Rachel muttered, but she hesitated.

"Rachel," her mother continued in her harried, worried voice, "That Rip person. He's... well, he's *bad*. Don't you see that? If you keep seeing him, he's just going to..." She wrung her hands, as if not knowing what to say next, as if a torrent of words wanted to fall from her lips but she didn't dare speak them. To speak them would make it actual, make it *real*, make it *her daughter*, and things like that didn't need to be discussed on Kookaburra Lane, no they did *not*.

"What, Ma? He's going to what?" Rachel struck what she thought of as her impatient pose, the one that said she was waiting for an answer she knew wasn't going to be the correct one. It was a mocking stance, a "yeah-let's-hear-*this-one*" but she also knew without knowing it that it was also defensive.

"He's going to get you *hurt*, Rachel, hurt or something else. Something worse." Fran's eyes began to tear, and that was something Rachel just couldn't handle. Every time her mother cried, she cried. She never knew if crying was calculating on her mother's part, like her own impatient pose, but she suspected.

She hated that she knew how alike she and her mother were—it was time for her to declare her own independence. If your life, your personality, is only made up of bits and pieces of your parents, how much of yourself is really you?

Rachel reached for the doorknob and her mother stopped her once again. Now, she didn't shout. Her voice was calm, metered, sad. "What happened to you, Rachel? What happened to the good girl who came home from school and did all her homework, huh? The girl who used to write poetry. That was beautiful poetry, Rachel. Why did you stop? Did I do something, or your father? Is that it?"

Rachel paused again, her lips trembling. She couldn't say *Nothing happened, Ma. For some reason, at some point, I decided I wanted something different than the nice, stable house on Kookaburra Lane. Nothing to do with you or Dad, I think. Just me. Oh, and I think you're right. I think Rip is dangerous, and he scares me, but he also excites me and I don't know why. And if I can't figure that one out, I'm sure not going to give it to you. I don't think you'd understand. I don't think anyone can.* She couldn't say those words, not even if she wanted to.

The bray of Rip's horn came from outside again. The short, sharp sound brought Rachel out of her reverie, clearing the confusing thoughts clouding her mind.

Aloud, she said, "Ma, I'm going out with Rip. That's it, end of story." She stepped out into the cool air of the night, closing the door of the sane, ordered life of Kookaburra Lane behind her. The black van at the end of the walk was waiting to swallow her, to envelop her, and to take her away from sanity and order. Rachel was on the edge, and though it scared her, she found she liked it.

* * *

Again, Tavin's Quarry, and this time Rip's friends had joined them. Howard Linneman was a fat kid Rachel remembered from one of her mandatory computer classes at Sheldon High. She recalled he hadn't been very popular, both his size and his affinity for Army gear keeping him out of the more popular circles, but he had been a genius at the computer. She also remembered Howard as being the kid who got into got into a fight with a sophomore one day last year and had ended up spraying the sophomore's eyes with mace until he screamed. Rachel didn't like Howard much.

He leaned back against the Quarry wall, the dog tags which hung from his neck glittering in the moonlight. He ran a hand through his spiky buzz cut and looked at Rachel. She didn't like the way he looked at her, especially when he had his glasses off. The glasses somehow humbled him, eased his features, made him somewhat normal. Without them, he looked like an ex-Army psychopath, and he leered at her with a half-grin plastered on his pudgy face.

"Hey Rachel," he said, as if trying to get her attention, even though she was looking right at him.

"What?" she asked, not wanting to know. Her legs dangled off the edge of Streak's Revenge, hanging a hundred feet over the black water pit below. She scissored her legs back and forth, banging her heels against the face of the ledge, and wondered crazily how it would feel to just jump, to fall all that way into the liquid abyss below. She thought about it, almost desperately, but in the end decided not to.

"Do you know what the difference between a serial killer and a mass murderer is?" He giggled happily and took the joint Rip handed him.

"You're stoned, Howard," she said, disgusted.

"Yeah, but that doesn't answer my question. Do *you* know the difference...?"

"No-brainer, Linneman," said Joan Parks, sitting next to Howard on the far side of Streak's Revenge. She took the joint from him and sucked smoke in. Rachel looked at her as she had at Howard, with contempt and repulsion. Joan, like Howard, would eventually go down in the hall of infamy in the annals of Sheldon High. When they were all juniors, Joan had tried to flush a freshman girl's head down the toilet in the ladies' room. She hadn't done it for any particular reason, just because she wanted to. There were also rumors that she was a dyke, but Rachel didn't care much either way. She didn't hate Joan for being a lesbian, she hated her because Joan was a bitch.

"Serial killer," Joan said slowly, "Kills her victims over time. A mass murderer kills 'em all at once." A series of pot-induced giggles followed, and she handed the joint back to Rip.

"What do you mean *her*?" Howard said, appearing actually angry. "All serial killers are guys, Parks."

"Wrong, Linneman," Rip said softly. The pot didn't seem to be affecting him as it was the others. He seemed calm, serene, almost sober. "Aileen Wuornos. Convicted serial killer in '92."

"Yeah, and you can also count Caril Fugate who went with Starkweather in the fifties, right?" Joan asked.

"More of a spree killer than a serial killer," Rip said, obviously becoming bored with the topic. He handed the joint to Rachel, who shook her head and buried her hands even further into her armpits. It was cold here tonight.

"Suit yourself," Rip muttered, and took another hit.

"Hey Rip," Howard whined, "Share around."

"I'll share when I want to, fat boy, now shut up." Howard did. Rip snuffed the joint, laced his hands behind his head, and asked of no one in particular, "What about a place?'

"What do you mean?" Joan asked, looking at Rip intently. Rachel saw her eyes were bloodshot.

"A place being a serial killer. Or maybe just a place being evil. Like, calling to evil. I heard about this house in Connecticut, this Berkley Street house, that made its owners murders. The last guy that lived there, a cop, said that there were monsters in the kitchen that made him do it."

A sharp wind glanced off the water below and carried up to Streak's Revenge. Rachel shivered, suddenly feeling cold all over.

"Or this place," Rip continued in that eerily serene voice. "Tavin's Quarry. Do you know how many people have been killed here. Killed... or disappeared?"

No one said a word. They all knew that Tavin's was a deathtrap. When it was first being mined for the granite that helped put Sheldon on the map, a freak rockslide killed a dozen men. That was in the standard syllabus at Sheldon Middle—every kid over ten knew about the Quarryman Tragedy. In the hundred years since, the Sheldon police had dragged over fifty bodies out of the water, or taken their dead, flattened bodies from the natural rock pier of Chicken's Paradise a hundred feet down. Kids who came in the fall to climb the slightly inclined rock walls of the Quarry or kids who came in midsummer to challenge each other to leap from higher and higher ledges. Kids who were found bloated and purple from having drowned, or mutilated nearly beyond recognition from connecting with the rocks.

Then there were the kids like Streak Atchison. The kids who were never found.

Rachel felt a dark rime of ice close around her heart as a thought barreled into her brain: *What happens to the kids they don't find? Where do they go?*

She looked down into the dark water below, that black gurgling maw, and found she didn't like her feet dangling off the edge anymore. The water had gained some quality, some sort of sentience, in her mind. It now looked somewhat... *hungry. Waiting.* For what? Maybe for one confused high school senior that may or may not taste spoiled? Could that be it?

Rachel yanked her feet up and moved against the rock wall between Rip and Howard.

"Gonna cry, Rach?" Howard asked, grinning, leering.

"You suck, freak," she said, angry both at the accusation and the fact that he was right. Suddenly, she *did* feel a little like crying.

What am I doing here? she asked herself mutely, desperately. *It's one in the morning, I'm freezing my ass off, sitting on a quarry ledge with two people I don't even like and a boyfriend—a* boyfriend—*who I don't even know I want to be with.* She looked over at Rip, who was staring out across Tavin's with a dark, unconnected gaze. Her mind slipped into a memory effortlessly, a terrifying scene she wanted to forget. She had been walking in Johnson's Woods with Rip out on the Quincy side of town. She was steeling herself for the probability of sex with him; even this soon, she had begun to loathe it with him. She had glanced over at him and seen that vague, disconnected look. Ahead of them a small white stray cat crossed their path.

"Rip?" she had asked, and all of a sudden he had rushed forward at the cat, screaming at the top of his lungs, his boot pistoning forward, catching the cat, sending it screeching, flying, and all Rachel could do was stand and watch, unbelieving. On some level, she had known he was capable of violence, but it had never manifested itself until that day, cloudy and upsetting. She had felt sick to her stomach. Her mother had asked her that night at dinner what was wrong, and she found she couldn't tell her.

Now, she inhaled a sharp, shuddery breath. *Maybe Mom was right. Maybe I should go back to poetry.*

Rachel's thoughts cut off abruptly as Rip stood up and sauntered to the edge of Streak's Revenge, where Rachel had sat, feet dangling precipitously, moments before.

"You know what I think is really funny?" he asked, not turning around. He paused, waiting for an answer, when Rachel finally responded.

"What's funny, Rip?"

"That we're all so freaked about death. It's gonna happen to everyone." He stopped, turned. The half-moon shone down on his face, casting it in the half-lunatic light of the potentially insane.

"Death is actually pretty funny. You guys know that? We're all gonna die, and nobody wants to accept it till it happens. Death is all that counts in the end. *That's* funny."

He walked toward them, and immediately Rachel knew that he was going to start kicking one of them, probably her, to the ground with his steel toed boots, and then stomp on her head over and over until her brains oozed out of her ears and blood spouted from her nose and her skull crunched like someone chewing popcorn and he would laugh his eerie, shriekish laugh and say to the others, "Isn't it *funny*, isn't it fucking *FUNNY*?"

But Rip, of course, did no such thing. He walked past them to the steep path by the side of the ledge, and began to climb the embankment to the top.

Maybe he'll do us all a favor by sliding and falling a hundred feet down, Rachel thought, only moderately surprised that the thought had no accompanying remorse.

None at all.

He didn't slip, and on the ride home, Rachel made a promise to herself that she would never see Rip again. He was getting too weird, too psychotic. Besides, she didn't like who he hung around with, and one of those people she didn't like was herself. Her mom had been right, she *had* become a different person. And though living with the danger of that different person had been fun for a while, at least until tonight, maybe, the act got old real fast. When she got home, she would wash off her makeup, throw away the thrash metal CDs she didn't really like, and apologize to her parents. She promised herself, on that long, silent ride home, that everything would go back to being how it was before Rip came into her life, as soon as she stepped out of that monstrous black van and back into her nice suburban house in Kookaburra Lane.

But even then, even in the depths of her resolve, she knew Rip's dark hold on her was still strong, and these were promises she wouldn't keep.

5 / Now

She climbs into the passenger seat and glances around her. This damned black van that rolled into her life and caused all this shit. She remembers when she first saw it, that fateful early summer day. The last day of junior year; Sheldon High would have to wait nearly three months before its resident girl poet re-entered its hallowed halls. She remembers thinking thoughts like that with bitterness, not for the first time feeling trapped in her place in life, feeling too structured, too ordered.

Then she had glanced across the parking lot and had seen the van, as ominous then as it is now, but then it had been somewhat sexy and mysterious. And she had seen its driver, with his long black hair like a heavy metal singer's and she had seen his deep, deep blue eyes even from across the parking lot, and realized without caring that she was excited by him. Him and the van.

She had wondered what it would be like to ride in it. Would it be dangerous, would it scare her? Suddenly, she felt a craving for that potential danger, for the thrill of being scared. Finally, she was faced with a way to break out of the school and the life.

She remembers going up to him and staring into those blue, blue eyes. How they pierced into her. How the seemed to glow. He had asked her if she wanted a ride home, and she said yes. He *had* driven fast, fast enough to shed that skin for a while, that quiet complacency of Kookaburra Lane, and when she got home she found she to do it again, again, to feel speed and power and danger and fear, that's what she wanted, that's what Rachel wanted.

Now she looks around her. The van doesn't have a back seat; when Joan and Howard came along they had to sit on the floor. The dashboard it plastered with those serial killer trading cards that had been banned in Massachusetts years before. Rip had glued them down with Krazy Glue, all his favorites: Charles Starkweather, Jeffrey Dahmer, Ted Bundy, David Berkowitz, Elmer Moody, John Wayne Gacy. Looking at the dashboard now makes her feel nauseous.

A brief shiver jets down her spine as she realizes that everyone who has ridden in the van is now dead, everyone except Rip and herself. Tonight, yes tonight, Rachel, even that would change.

Another chill grasps her and she thinks about the others. She thinks about the dead she knew as alive just a night before.

6 / THEN

The promise Rachel made to herself wasn't entirely forgotten, but it wasn't exactly remembered, either. She was going to see Rip again tonight. She couldn't explain it to herself, but the thought of him, that danger about him, still tugged at her. She didn't want to see him tonight, this Saturday night when she could be doing a million other things, but in a way she did want to go. It was like a bad instinct, a small rabbit following the scent of the wolf, even though the trail ends in certain death.

"You're not going, Rachel," her father said sternly as she hurried down the stairs. The horned outside blatted again. Rip didn't like waiting.

"Now you listen to me, young lady," Lawrence McHugh continued in that same stern voice, but the tone was hollow and easily shattered. Her mom had been a little better at this, but when it came right down to it, the McHughs weren't strong-willed people.

I wish he'd ground me, Rachel's subconscious buzzed. She crossed the living room to the front door. *I wish he'd grab me, send me to my room.*

But he didn't, and momentarily she felt torn. She didn't want to see Rip and his stoner friends again, not after the weird way Rip acted last night, but she couldn't *not* go, either. It would mean backing down, caving into her parents, going back to that old life, and she hated that idea more than looking into Rip's pale, dangerous eyes and wondering what was behind them.

* * *

Climbing up into the passenger side of the van, Rachel glanced around to see if Howard and Joan were joining them tonight. Rachel had a vague idea that one or both of them would stay home tonight after the way Rip had acted at Tavin's last night.

Especially Howard. Howard was scared of Rip, she knew, but she also knew the power, the attraction Rip held. Howard acted angry, mean, but he was a coward and he was weak. Maybe she was, too. And Rip had something—some dark charisma—that made them want to gather around him. So she wasn't really surprised to see them both here, powerless to steel themselves against Rip's dangerous will. Just like her.

She was, however, surprised at the sight of a third person, squished against the back door between Howard and Joan. He was a tall, gangly kid Rachel remembered vaguely from a computer class she had taken the year before. Like Howard, he was dressed in Army gear, including the dog tags and scuffed boots. What was his name? Rachel tried to remember, but her mind sidestepped; Jason? Jared?

"Who...?" she began, and Howard cut her off.

"Jeremy Hollis, Rach. Thought we'd let him come along for the ride." He giggled, that high squealing giggle that Rachel knew hid Howard's brand of fear. Joan joined the laughter, but her eyes betrayed her, shooting furtive glances at the back of Rip's head as he drove. Jeremy himself raised a small hand and uttered a diminutive "Hello."

Rachel waved back and turned toward. Something was definitely wrong here. An air of fear-laced tension had permeated the van, transforming it into something like a gas-chamber on wheels. Joan and Howard were acting strangely, even for them, and it seemed even young, naïve Jeremy Hollis sensed something slightly off.

Why is he here? Rachel wondered. *He's one of the smart kids. He spends his entire day in the computer labs because he aces all his classes.* She turned again to look at the three in the back of the van. They all stared ahead, quiet. No one spoke, not even Howard, who usually wouldn't shut up if you paid him.

Jeremy looked very small against the back doors of Rip's giant van. Very small, and very vulnerable.

What is he doing here?

Her mind shot back violently, *You used to be one of the smart kids, too, Rachel. Remember that? Now look where you are.*

She turned back to take in the rolling of the road, stunned. Her legs felt atrophied, her arms stiff rods. Suddenly, she wanted to be out of here. Take Jeremy

Hollis by the hand and leap out the back door. Resume honors classes at Sheldon High. Write poetry. Play chess. Be a smart kid again. Could she do that?

The van stopped and Rip dropped a heavy hand on her thigh, stroking it roughly. "We're here, babe," Rip sad, and grinned devilishly.

The thoughts coalescing in her head leapt out like scared rabbits from cages. A pain too deep to be physically felt crept into her heart. Rip smiled. "You comin'?"

"Yeah," Rachel sighed, staring into those dark eyes. "I guess so."

Rip Treymoore left the van, and Rachel followed.

* * *

Looking down at Jeremy as he climbed under the fence, Rachel found herself wondering why Jeremy dressed so much like Howard. He even had the buzz cut down cold. She laughed humorlessly at the absurdity of it.

If you want to mimic someone here, why Howard and not Rip? Howard was a follower with a bad macho act. The Army clothes belied his true, frightened nature, and even taking the glasses off to look like a psychopath wore off after a while. Why Howard?

Bad choice, kid, she thought pityingly, and shook her head.

"You wanna help me wipe off this dirt, kid?" Joan asked Jeremy shyly, bringing up one of his hands with hers and placing it on one of the gentle swells of her sweater. Rachel heard Jeremy gasp silently, and she almost laughed herself.

"Come on, let me show you where we go," Joan said in a sweet little-girl voice Rachel had never heard before. For some reason, it scared her.

"What's she doing with him?" asked Rachel, as Joan led Jeremy to the embankment and down toward Streak's Revenge.

"Oh, we're just having some fun with the kid, Rachel. Don't soak your tampons, right, Rip?"

"Yeah, fatboy. Now shut up." Howard's grin fell off, and he stared at Rip just as Rachel supposed she had in the van. A thought plunged into her mind, unwarranted and unprepared for:

Jeremy worships Howard because Howard was one of the smart kids, too. Some way, somehow, Howard made it into Rip's little group, and Jeremy sees that as some type of ascension. Maybe Jeremy thinks that if Rip accepted Howard, he has a chance of getting in, too. Maybe he has a shot of being one of us.

On the heels of that, *Why would anyone want to be one of us?* In a blind streak, her mind answered itself. *The control of fear equals the control of power, Rachel. That's the only truth here. And you better believe Rip knows it, too.*

Numbly, she followed as Rip and Howard also headed down the embankment.

When they arrived at Streak's Revenge, Rachel saw that Joan was running a light finger slowly in circles on Jeremy's chest. She was whispering something to him, too quietly for Rachel to hear. Jeremy stared ahead with a blank look in his eyes, and a confused smile twitching at his lips. He breathed shallow, shuddery breaths, and in the dark Rachel thought she could see a slight lump of erection in the folds of his jeans.

"Why...?" Rachel began, but Rip cut her off.

"Do you have your lighter, fatboy?" he asked of Howard, and Howard obediently handed it over. Rip lit it. In the deep glow of the flame, Rip's face appeared gaunt and tight, like that of a corpse's.

"Who wants to take a swim? Rip asked calmly, and somewhere in the woods behind the quarry face, an owl hooted as if in response.

"Isn't it a little *cold*, Rip?" Rachel asked, and a shiver shot through her. All of a sudden, it *did* seem colder.

"No way," Joan said, but there was a minute tremble in her voice. Rachel stared at her in disbelief. Joan was scared.

Why don't any of us say anything? Rachel thought, but her mouth felt gummed shut.

"Water's just right," Howard added and grinned toothily. His zits were solar flares erupting from his pale cheeks.

"Um, I didn't bring any shorts," Jeremy responded quietly, and to Rachel it looked as if the Army jacket he wore was suddenly too big on him. He looked losing at a game of War.

But they weren't playing, and she knew it.

"You don't need shorts, man," Rip said soothingly. In a panther-quick flurry of movement, Rip shot out a hand and grabbed Jeremy's arm, gripping tightly. Howard grabbed the other arm. Joan got a handful of olive drab Army jacket.

"H-Hey," Jeremy said, now terrified. "H-Hey, come on."

Rachel shrank back against the quarry wall, pressed flat, gripped in a thrall of terror so great she couldn't breathe. Her eyes widened, her pulse leapt. A scream threatened, but only a rasp came forth.

"You wanna hang with us, computer boy, you gotta swim with the sharks." Rips voice was low, dark. "There's only one way in, boy, and one way out. Get ready to fly." From five feet away, Rachel heard Jeremy's air catch, in a horrific sob. Then, piercingly, echoing across the quarry walls and in her ears, Jeremy shrieked.

"I CAN'T SWIM!"

Simultaneously, Joan and Howard let go of the boy.

Rachel rushed forward, adrenaline pumping, crying, "No!"

Laughing demonically, Rip thrust out, sending Jeremy screaming outward, plunging into that dark abyss, falling down, down.

Rachel closed her eyes tightly, waiting in terrified silence for the heavy splash, but it never came. Instead, a sickening *thump-squelch* rushed at them like a poisoned moan. Rachel rushed to the edge and saw.

Jeremy Hollis had landed a good six feet from the edge of Chicken's Paradise where water met rock. He lay in a mangled, crumpled heap, brilliant splashes of blood soaking into the jagged rocks around him. It seemed, in the moonlight, that Rachel could see everything.

Jeremy Hollis was dead.

"Poor guy," Rip said, and turned. "I guess he couldn't fly after all." He walked toward the path that led away from the ledge. He looked back at them. "You guys coming with me?"

Howard rushed at him. For the first time, Rachel saw something other than fear and adoration in his eyes. She thought she might be seeing hate.

"You just *killed* a kid, Rip! *Killed* him! All that blood, Rip, *did you see all that blood*?" Rip slapped him across the face, a meaty clap.

"I've seen more than that before, fatboy, now shut up. You're getting hysterical." Then, louder, "I said, are you guys coming with me?"

Rachel first thought of it then, of doing to Rip what he had done to Jeremy Hollis. At that moment, though, it was only the germination of an idea, a possibility that may or may not later come into fruition.

7/Now

Now, it has become her reality.

Because she'd been wrong before. Control of fear may equal control of power, but that wasn't the only truth. In this world, in the world of Rip's psychopathic mind in which she had lived, fear equaled power, but power, in turn, equaled death.

The power in fear, the power of death. The only two constants. Rip had been in control far too long.

But now, it was her turn.

8 / THEN

When Rip dropped her off earlier (kissing her firmly with clammy lips), she'd been sure she would burst through the front door and tell her parents everything, from the night she sacrificed her virginity to the lunatic murder of Jeremy Hollis. She planned to sit them down on the living room couch and spill out everything, sobbing but relieved to have it out.

But when she got inside, she found all the lights off, and both parents asleep upstairs in their bedroom. Standing outside their door, peeking in through the cracked door, she felt any courage and determination ooze out of her body like a rank odor. No, she would not tell them tonight, not when they looked so peaceful. Would she tell them tomorrow? Maybe. Would she tell them ever?

Her bed, at first, seemed hard and cold, as if made of cement. Wide-eyed and shaking, she'd been positive that she wouldn't be able to sleep. That prediction, too, proved false. Laying her head down on her pillow she fell asleep almost instantaneously.

She awoke with a start six hours later to the sound of a low, dragging noise outside her bedroom window.

Rrrrrrrraaaaaaaaaayyyyyyyyy... Quiet, almost delicate, floating in the breeze.

She sat up, clutching her bed sheets. The noise came again, louder now, and it wasn't a noise but a *voice*, an unintelligible drawl of half-awake sleep-tones.

Rrrrrrraaaaaaaaayyyyyyychuuuuuuuuullllll...

Her heart skipped crazily; she stared in transfixed horror at the screened window across the room. A light wind shuffled dry leaved below in a hiss. Goosebumps knotted tightly all over her flesh.

Don't get up, her mind commanded sharply. *Don't move. Hide under your covers until that noise, that noise that knows your name, goes away.*

Her feet swung out and connected with the cold hardwood floor. A brief shudder racked her body. Trembling, she shuffled across to the window, as if hypnotized. She needed to know, had to see. Who was out there, calling her from under her window at quarter to five in the morning? Was it Rip? Who? What?

Hhhhuuuurrrrrryyyy Rrrrrrraaaaaaaachuuuuullllll...

The noise, the *voice*, was closer. Gritty, choked.

Closer.

A creeping undersmell had leaked in through the screen, dark and pungent, like deep-cellar rot. Suddenly, it was everywhere, inescapable. She wanted to plug her nose, to run and hide, to move somewhere other than toward that window, toward that voice.

Reaching the window, she gripped the sill, pressing her nose against the metallic-smelling screen, and trying to peer out into the yard below.

"Hello?" she squeaked, and the hand ripped through the screen in a fury, clutching her wrist. It was cold, damp, a perversion of flesh. And it was *strong*, holding onto her wrist like a vice. Rachel stared at it, mouth gaping, mute horror lodged in her throat. Fingernails dug into her skin, drawing blood and securing its grip.

The hand closed tighter, and yanked forward. It was trying to pull whatever body it was connected to up, up and in, or...

Or trying to pull her out.

The thought triggered her brain, loosening it. Her shriek came forth in a fevered bolt, bright and high. Blinding terror held her mind as the hand held her wrist, screaming hard, screaming loud enough to piece the night.

Unthinkingly, she yanked back, bringing the wrist attached to the hand in, scraping it soundlessly against the frame. Pale white skin shaved off in bloodless curls. She reached up, grabbing the top of the open window itself. With all the strength in her free arm, she brought it down, shattering the window, projecting glass everywhere.

The second thud of the night echoed up to her, a plump crash onto the dead leaves and grass below. She fell to the floor, clutching her bleeding wrist. The screams had evaporated; all that came now were clenching sobs.

Moments passed. Her parents rushed into her room, throwing the door back hard enough to leave an indentation from the doorknob on the wall. Their arms, safe and warm, enveloped her.

"What happened, honey?" her father asked. "Was it a dream?"

"D-d-down," she answered softly. "The yard."

Her father looked to the screen, saw the rip, and frowned. Stepping carefully over the broken glass, he raised the window and the screen, looking out and shaking his head slowly.

Turning back, he said, concerned, "There's nothing down there now, honey. What did you see?"

Rachel cried, burying her face into her mother's shoulder, soaking the arm of her robe.

9/Now

They leave the van quietly by an epileptic street-light down on Quarry Road. It's dark here; the path they follow is more memory than eyesight, and Rachel thinks this is probably better. The dark frightens her, but the thought of Rip piecing together what she has planned by some open look on her face terrified her, and now she welcomes the dark.

She thinks back to that night in her room. Was it only last night? She fears the memory of that hand—Rip's hand—tightening on her will follow her into her nightmares for the rest of her life. The somehow moist feel of it, like he's been licking his palms. Had she really let those hands touch her body, touch it everywhere? Yes. Yes, she had. And that thought makes her want to puke.

They reach the fence and she can see the Quarry from here. She sighs as Rip squirms under the fence, her hands gripping the chain link. A lone tear courses down her cheek. She wants to ask why but figures it fruitless. There are no answers now, only actions.

She begins to crawl under the fence herself, sniffling a little.

10/THEN

Rachel woke and went downstairs to the kitchen, yawning. After last night, she knew something had to be done. She knew that as a fact now. No more shades of gray anymore. And she would have to start by telling her parents.

Her dad sat at the kitchen table, reading his newspaper, the Sheldon *Herald*. She glanced at the cover, and stopped, stopped dead when she saw the headline.

TWO TEENS DEAD, ONE MISSING; SHELDON POLICE BAFFLED

Her dad looked up, saw her standing there, and began to ask if anything was wrong. She didn't answer, couldn't answer, instead just grabbed the paper from him and scanned the article.

After the events of last night in her room, she'd put the death of Jeremy Hollis in the back of her brain. But there his picture was, screaming from the front page of the Sheldon *Herald* like an accusation. But his was not the only one, oh no, Jeremy Hollis was not the only one dead.

Accompanying the full-color picture of Jeremy were those of Joan Parker and Howard Linneman, flanking his photograph as they had flanked his person in the back of Rip's van the night before.

The article went on to state that sometime in the night, someone had broken into Howard and Joan's bedrooms. Both teens were found in their beds, their heads brutally struck with some blunt instrument until they died. Sharp chunks of granite had been found lodged in what remained of their skulls.

Jeremy Hollis was missing.

Rachel was unable to read further. She sat down hard, shaking uncontrollably. The police hadn't yet been able to connect the deaths and the disappearance, mainly because Jeremy belonged to a wildly different social clique. They weren't outright saying Jeremy had also been killed, but they hinted strongly that there may be a third in conjunction with the first two, and it may only be a matter of time before they find another teenager with his head smashed in.

Rachel, though, started piecing everything together then. After all, she had been there when the killer pushed Jeremy over the edge, and she had been there when he had tried to climb into her bedroom so he could bludgeon her to death too. What had he done with Jeremy's body? Gone back to dump it in the water? Bury it? What?

Her boyfriend, the one person she had allowed inside her, had killed three people and had tried for a fourth. Her.

Go to the police, Rachel, she thought, *or tell your parents. He's got to be stopped, he needs to be stopped.*

Her mind pounced on the idea, and she opened her mouth to tell her Dad, when something inside clicked. No, not the police, because she was sort of an accomplice to Jeremy's death. And not her parents, because they wouldn't understand why she had done nothing. No, no, this would have to be her doing, her alone. She was the only one left.

She had to murder Rip. Plain and simple, she had to kill her boyfriend. How wonderful that thought seemed. God, that was sick, but it did seem wonderful. Maybe she had caught some of Rip's psychosis, his mania. But now, that didn't seem important.

All that seemed important was taking Rip to the edge of Streak's Revenge, and pushing him into that dark unknown below.

11/Now

She feels nervous, tingly. She doesn't feel the same sense of freedom she had felt at the breakfast table that morning, across from her father, holding his paper in tight hands. Instead, she has a feeling of lightness about her head. Could it be that she's high? High on the anticipation of murder? Is this how Rip felt last night?

They reach the steep path leading down to the progression of ledges. Rip saunters down to the third, Streak's Revenge, and steps to the edge. Rachel remains slightly behind, looking out over the Quarry. It really is beautiful out here, would be beautiful if not for the angle of her view. From Streak's Revenge. So much had been lost here. It hadn't just been Rip robbing her of her innocence and Jeremy Hollis of his life. It's this whole place, this dirty place, this dark place. Her mind shifts uncontrollably to the names of the past, names she has heard throughout her life in connection with this Quarry. Jaquelyn Toivenen, Jason Moscate, Jeffrey McAuley, dozens more, so many. Falls, murders, suicides, rockslides. This place is full of death, bloated with death.

Just one more, she thinks, *just one more and I don't have to be a part of it anymore.* She steps forward silently, and then Rip speaks, not turning around.

"Hear about Howard and Joan, babe?" he asks, almost whispering it. She stops. What is he doing? Toying with her? Does he know what she plans? "Kind of funny about them, huh?"

"Y-yeah," she answers, now frightened for herself as well as frightened of what she is doing. "Yeah, kind of funny."

"*Death.* It's so fucking funny, babe, remember when I said that? One second you're sound asleep, and the next your head is beaten in with a rock. I wonder who did it? Do you?"

"Do what?' Her voice trembles.

"Wonder who did it? Wonder who bashed their skulls in until they were nothing but oatmeal. I wanted to know if you wondered who did it."

"No," she whispers steadily. Her eyes flare in anger and fury. "No, because I *know* who killed them."

"Oh yeah?" he asks, not turning. "Who?"

You know damn well who, asshole, she thinks, her fear dissipating, leaving a cold bullet rage that consumes her. At the last, rushing moment, perhaps he realizes what she's doing, and he turns, his arms up.

Then the push. The plummet. The scream downward as Jeremy had screamed the night before, as Howard and Joan had undoubtedly tried to scream, as she had screamed herself. Her ears fill up with it, her body quakes with it. A nocturne of terror grips her as the dark thud carries up from the bottom ledge, breaking the scream in half, shattering the night.

Then, she allows herself to cry. She holds herself and weeps out over Tavin's Quarry, over all the death, and she now discovers, no, it isn't funny after all.

12/THEN

In the kitchen, while Rip sat hormonally in her living room, Rachel wrote a note to her parents:

Mom and Dad,

I know I've been a real jerk in these past few weeks, but I swear it's almost over. I'm breaking up with Rip tonight, saying goodbye to him forever. After seeing those pictures of his friends in the paper today, I realized that Rip's life is dangerous, and I don't want to be a part of it anymore. Thanks for putting up with me, and thanks for being there.

Love,

Your daughter Rachel

13/Now

Poor guy, Rachel thinks, *I guess he couldn't fly after all.*

Now she sits, legs dangling from the edge of Streak's Revenge. Looking down, she can just make out the shape of Rip's body, but it's mostly masked in moonlight and shadow. She doesn't really care. All she cares about now is that he's dead, and now life can go in.

She's planning, mapping out how she will restart her life from this point on. After she leaves here, she will begin the long walk to the Sheldon Center subway stop, where she can catch a bus home to Kookaburra Lane. She will say how she and Rip went down to the Quarry, and how she broke up with him. How he slapped her across the face. And how she left him, telling him to have a good life. The next morning, they will find his broken body as they hadn't found Jeremy's, and deem Rip's death a suicide. Rip killed himself over the loss of his girl. And that, my friends, *is* funny, because Rachel is perhaps the only person alive that knows Rip could never have feelings that deep for anything but death itself.

She sits, contemplating her future, looking out across the Quarry. She wants to think more about constructing her life, but is that the only reason why she stays? No. She also sits here because now she is unsure. Something is wrong, some vital piece of the puzzle she forgot or simply doesn't see. Could she have been wrong about Rip murdering Joan and Howard? Or it being Rip's hand clawing her way through her screen last night? Or Rip coming back here and getting rid of Jeremy Hollis's body? Could she have been mistaken about anything? Everything?

She looks up over the Quarry, the essential beauty of the place juxtaposed by its essential ugliness, and she stands. It doesn't matter now if she was wrong or not, she supposes. It's done, Rip is dead, everyone is dead.

"Goodbye," she whispers, but she doesn't know who she is saying it to. She turns to walk up the narrow path that leads to the top of the Quarry, when she sees someone—*something*—standing there and she screams.

"Raaaaccchhhuuuullll...." the thing says, shambling toward her. Its face is a bloodied wreck, its body sunken and mangled. One eyeball hangs on its mashed cheek from a thin, dangling vein. And it is wearing an olive drab Army jacket, a little too big for him.

"Oh... oh my G..." Rachel's breath becomes shuddery, wracked. She is seeing Jeremy Hollis here, and now everything falls into place. Not Rip, it wasn't Rip. Jeremy had killed Howard, then Joan, then had come for her. The hand that had come through her screen...

"No blood! I scraped it and there was no blood!"

Jeremy lurches toward her, slouching and reaching. She takes a step back, closer to the edge of Streak's Revenge. Her mind is a black, insane raven beating furiously against the walls of her skull. Somewhere across the Quarry, an owl begins to hoot furiously.

"Rrrrrraaaaaaacccchhhhuuuuuullll..." and she reached the edge, crying, moaning, and that is when something grabs her ankle and she screams. She looks behind her, looks down, and sees it is Rip. Beyond him, down in the black water, she sees skulls emerging from the depths. Dead people, dead teenagers, those among the missing. As she soon would be.

Rachel looks back, looks up, and shrieks into Jeremy Hollis's dead, gore-splattered face. Then the dead hand clutching her ankle yanks her back, and she tumbles, watching the dead rise from the cold, dark, evil water at crazy angles. She screams, and falls, and when she reaches the bottom she is ravaged.

Some unknown time later, the waters calm and the owl stops its crazed call.

Tavin's Quarry falls silent.

Screw You

Murder. Such an ugly term for such a beautiful thing.

Maybe I should introduce myself, but I'm not one for formality. I'm the guy who pumps gas down to the Sunoco station on Brawfurst Road. The one with the red baseball cap and the uniform shirt with the name tag torn off. I pump gas and help people on their way. I smile as I take their money—a big, white, earnest smile. I wonder where they are going, and who they will see when they get there.

Sometimes I don't wonder.

Sometimes I look into their blank, stupid faces and think about the corkscrew hidden under the porno mags in my dresser.

I guess there never really was a time I decided killing was right for me. The first one happened when I was fourteen. It was 1968, the summer of love. I remember hearing Tommy James and the Shondells on the radio a lot. None of that "Mony Mony" noise crap either—it was the soft rhythm of "Crimson and Clover." I was out in the woods behind the hockey rink with a girl I knew from school. Her name was Brenda something—as the years go by, it's so hard, so hard to keep track of so many.

We weren't in love, oh no, far from it. We had just started talking a few weeks before then, in private. She was wildly interested in sex; that sort of thing didn't much appeal to me. But she was all for it, so I said what the hell.

We met after school that day (after school, now there's a fucking foreign phrase! I was a freshman in high school then. Goddamn how time flies!) behind Kapinski's Intermediate Hockey Rink. I had brought champagne I stole from the back of the fridge because I figured it was what Brenda expected. To celebrate or something, you know? Champagne and my transistor radio—a double shot of Tommy James was coming up as we walked off the path into a clearing. She was all hot for me, grabbing at the front of my jeans even before we got to a hidden spot. When we did get there, I slid my hand under her sweater. She wasn't wearing anything beneath that and her nipples were hard and sharp. The rest of her, though was soft, too soft.

Tommy James came on. I still remember how sweet those words sounded rolling out of the transistor like silk on top of a summer day. I remember her grabbing at my fly, trying to unzip me, and her hand fumbling across my pocket. There was something there much harder than what she would find nestled like a worm in my Jockeys. She asked what it was.

"Corkscrew," I answered, and her face was dull and stupid and confused. I reached into the pocket to pull it out, felt the coolness of the marble handle turn warm in my sweaty hand. The long, steel screw poked out, glimmering, between my middle and ring finger. "See?"

Then it just happened. I didn't even know I was going to do it. But as I brought the corkscrew down and slashed a bloody scarlet line diagonally across her face, I began to understand that this was the real reason why I went down there that day. She wanted sex, I wanted to kill her. In that, I suppose I was greedy, but her part of the bargain wasn't working for me, either. She was not turning me on, not at all, not one bit.

But I'll tell you something: after I tore her face to shreds, and was covering up her body with the leaves, I discovered something. At one point during the excitement I came—and I think I might have come twice. I don't really know, and it bugs me a little, but that's okay. I knew right then that killing was what my life was there for.

* * *

I realized right away that I couldn't repeat myself. I recognize my status as a serial killer. I accept that. What is important for me is that no one else knows I'm a serial killer, either personally or from the work I do. I always use the corkscrew; that never changes. But the methodology does, and the type I kill does. Sometimes I go into bookstores and browse through those books on serial killers. It's so ludicrous. They get caught because of one of two reasons. One, they get sloppy. That won't happen with me, because it's my belief that if a guy loves his job he should take a certain pride in it. And I feel a real sense of accomplishment whenever I murder someone. Sure, it's fun, but it's a lot of work. Because I *do* love it, and want to continue it, I can't get careless. There's no room for mistakes in what I do.

The other reason they get caught is because they're so damn predictable. I respect the federal agents and police officers who catch serial killers, because it's damned hard to respect the other side when they get as repetitive as they do. The feds can make a profile on the killer based on type of murders and type of victims. There's such a thing as *forensics*. Well, if you're going to kill only overweight Caucasian males, you're eventually going to get caught. And if you keep taking a certain trophy or leaving a certain clue behind, you're eventually going to get caught.

Not me. Anyone, anywhere: that's my motto. Never play the game with the same team too long, and never let anyone know it's the work of a single person. Kill them and mutilate them to the point they can't discern the weapon, never do the same type of person twice, and don't stay in one area for very long. It's so fucking simple. But these guys who kill don't do it for the reasons I do it. They do it because of compulsions and obsessions. Eventually those compulsions and obsessions are going to get the better of you, and you will hang yourself.

I don't want to go off on a psychological thing here, because I'm not much for psychology. But I will say this: those other serial killers have something going on upstairs that's just a little off. I'm not saying that they're all insane, but a good bunch of them are, and the rest are skewed just enough so that it amounts to the same. Not me. I'm as sane as the next guy, providing the next guy doesn't happen to be Charles Manson.

I do it because I love it. It makes me happy. It's not as often as I'd like, but no one gets what he or she wants as often as they'd like. You just have to what you can to balance off your life so as to accommodate your fun. It's the way I live, anyway.

But I have to say, not all of them are great. For instance, I like them to shut up while I'm doing it. Sometimes they go into this really cool catatonic shock when they realize they're being killed—their eyes glaze over and they drool a little bit. God, that gets me horny. And then it's silent, deadly, and quick—I get my rocks off and they slide into oblivion.

But this one time I had this guy, six feet tall, around two hundred pounds. He wasn't fat, either—that was all what appeared to be football muscle. It was interesting, too, because it was the first and only time I'd ever done anything like that at work. It was a close call, and I'll never do anything like it again. What happened was this:

I was getting ready to close up at the gas station. My boss had gone home hours before, and the night had come down quickly, quickly. The moon was high like a sickle when the guy drove up, all in a hurry. He drove a white sedan—a BMW I think. When he got out, I felt a little twinge in the back of my mind. Most of the time I just pick and choose my victims at random, but sometimes the little twinge perks up. Usually that's an indicator that I'll have some real fun with this one—like every motivated person in the world, I love a challenge. This guy, dressed in a T-shirt and black jeans, seemed to present a challenge.

I must have had some type of premonition that morning, too, because I'd brought the corkscrew to work with me. I don't do that often, just when I think I might go prowling that night. And it was so damn perfect, there at the beginning.

He needed to use the bathroom. He didn't need any gas, he said, and he saw I was packing it in, but he didn't want to have to shit in the woods. We both had a little laugh at that, and I said sure, and went for the key. As I got it (it was a key which dangled from a long chain attached to a gigantic wooden fob), I also reached into my backpack and got the corkscrew. I'd had the thing for years and had mastered the art of taking it from my backpack and slipping it into my jeans pocket in one quick maneuver. I left the office, jogging a little to give the key to him. He looked so silly, standing there in the crisp air of October, hopping from foot to foot. It was all really funny to me, but I was getting a little excited. The butterflies were twittering around my tummy, and I had a good feeling about this.

* * *

He let himself into the bathroom, a single small room which smells of urine and waste. I checked the road to see if there were any cars coming from either way, but Brawfurst Road is pretty quiet after six or so. I dug out my keyring from my other pocket and selected the bathroom key—the one given to employees in case of emergency.

I was as quiet as humanly possible slipping that key into the lock, and that's what saved me, maybe. When I flung open the door, the guy had his pants around his ankles and his head in his hands, elbows leaving red marks on his bare, hairy legs. He looked up, shocked, and I kicked the door closed behind me. I heard the automatic lock click home. The smell of shit rose in the air, but the hormones raging through me killed it. I tore the corkscrew from my jeans pocket, gripped it, and plugged it into the guy's chest before he could move.

Then, he began to scream. Goddamn, I hate that noise. At least it wasn't a high-pitched, womanly scream—it was low and shocked and terrified. I plunged the corkscrew in again, this time in the fleshy part right above his armpit. That was when, still screaming that billowing scream, he began to fight me.

As I've said, it was a small room—barely large enough for two people. The walls were this depressing beige and the overhead flickering fluorescent didn't help much. But my mind was flying high by then, and I discovered something strange. I was scared, and I was getting off on it. It wasn't something I'd want all the time—I figured I'd get bored by fear soon enough. But now I could somehow appreciate the terror in my victims' eyes as they tumble into darkness. And, in recognizing that element, appreciate it even more. Relish it.

* * *

He grabbed me by my shoulders before I could stab again and he threw me against the wall. I'm no physics major, but I believe you need to have at least a little throwing room to make any kind of impact. Fortunately for me, the tightly enclosed space wasn't all that good for battering. For stabbing, however, it was ideal.

He only got that one offensive move in, and now, looking back on it, I wish he would have gotten more. As I've said, that fear was exquisite, and I'm sad to say it was the last time I really felt it. After he threw me to the wall, well, I kind of lost it. I punched the corkscrew into his eye, watching mucusy white liquid dribble all over the haft. He kept screaming, and I kept telling him to shut the fuck up. Into his nose, his cheek, his other eye, his chest. Screaming, screaming—edging up toward insane cat warbling.

Eventually I realized the only way to stop him from screaming was to shove the corkscrew into his throat. I waited a moment though, looking over my creation— bloody, half-naked, mutilated beyond belief. I looked at him for a moment and smiled. I know it's dirty, and it shouldn't feel this good. But it does, it does. God, I love to kill.

After I finished vivisecting his throat and neck, I looked up and realized I had a problem. The walls of the bathroom, the guy lying slumped on the toilet, and yours truly were all slathered in blood. Also, I hadn't worn rubber gloves -- which I *always* wear. They're really good at fingerprint analysis these days. It took a few moments of quick thinking, but I soon came up with a plan.

The tool kit in the office had three X-Acto knives. I selected one and returned to the bathroom. There, I proceeded to use the only instrument of destruction besides my corkscrew I've ever used—sawing into the guy's flesh and bone as hard as I could. When I was done with him, I went to work on myself: slashing up my face, my arms, and tearing into my coat. The only serious mark I made was a deep gash in my chest, and it hurt like a motherfucker. Still, I once again felt that raising of consciousness, that endorphin high. This is what *they* feel: crimson and clover, over and over. But it was neither the time nor the place to come again. I'd done plenty of that during the melee with the gent from the BMW.

I called 911 with my story of a crazy guy in a pickup slashing his way down Brawfurst Road. There were just few enough residents on Brawfurst and just enough slashes on me for my story to stick. No one ever checked under the stack of newspapers in the newspaper dispenser; if they had they would have found the corkscrew. And no one questioned the amount of X-Acto knives in the toolbox; my boss never does any actual work and I'm the only one that knew there wasn't actually one missing. The one I'd used I simply cleaned off and put back. It was simple, when you got right down to it.

Simple, but it put a shock into me. It was almost two weeks before I killed again.

That was the only real bad time, and bad is kind of a harsh word for it. Unique. That might be better. The end result remains the same: I got away with it and I keep getting away with it.

I don't have a sense of higher purpose, you know. I'm not on an ego bender. I don't feel as if I'm better than anyone else, and therefore have to kill my lessers. Not me.

I'm just a guy who has a lot of fun with his given talent. Some guys can paint, some guys can play Trivial Pursuit. I kill. It turns me on, it makes me happy, it makes me feel a sense of a job well done.

I also pump gas. Look for me, in my red cap and my uniform without a name. I'll give you a smile while humming a song—something from the sixties.

I'm a corker.

The Curious Life of Dennis Morbach

It is *so* not fun being a werewolf.

You'd think it would be, right? The whole "creature of the night" thing and all. But no: vampires have that nailed down. You ever see *Lost Boys*? *Interview With a Vampire*? Fucking *Twilight*? Sure, everyone gets all sad and angsty at the end, but until then, vampires are all cool and shit. Name one movie where were-wolves are cool. See, you can't. And don't you dare say *Teen Wolf*, don't you *dare*. I think that if the werewolf life consisted of van-surfing and listening to the Beach Boys and winning basketball tournaments, I might be a lot happier. No, they get *Fright Night*. We get *The Howling*. They get freakin' *Dracula*, for chrissake! We get Michael Landon. Pre-*Highway to Heaven* Michael Landon, even.

You also wanna know what vampires get? A club. That's right. There's this whole vampire club that meets like once a week in Austin. No shit. It's at a regular bar, this place called Jake's, and every Saturday, the owner closes it down for the regulars and opens it up for vampires. And from what my friend Beth tells me, the guy's totally not a vampire himself, so he's totally Renfielding, which is just not cool. Even Beth says. You almost wanna tell the cops, but like, what are the cops gonna do? Even if they believed me, I'd be sending a whole squad of Austin's best in blue into this whole vamp nest, and that's never pretty. (Yeah, I'm not supposed to call it a "nest," either, Beth says. Not PC. Sometimes Beth really gets on my nerves.)

You know what also sucks about being a werewolf? The whole right to choose thing. You're a vampire, it's all, yay, I'm a bloodsucker, but then you get to make the decision about whether you're evil or not. No kidding, Beth told me the whole thing. I guess back in the 1800s, there was like no way out of it. You're a vampire, so you're evil. Somewhere along the line, something changed. Bloodlines thinned out or something, or got too mixed with human blood. I don't know. This is all secondhand news. Anyway, no matter how it started off, now if you're a vampire you can be pretty much normal, except for having to drink blood and no daylight. Or church, I guess. But if you're a werewolf, three nights a month it's all fuzzy wuzzy was a wolf, bark at the moon, and yum let's rend some flesh. I guess maybe it's a blessing or something that I don't remember thing one about what I do when I change. That's what Beth calls it, a blessing. I'm not so sure. I mean, if I'm not gonna have any say in me changing, I'd at least like to know what happens when I'm wolfed out, you know? I only remembered everything afterward once, and that was a completely different thing, so I'm not even gonna count it.

I don't even remember how I *became* a werewolf, isn't that the lamest thing you ever heard? I'm guessing it was on that trip up to Possum Kingdom Mom and Dad took me to two years ago. Fishing! Dad said. Camping! Mom said. It'll be fun and rustic! That's the word they kept using, rustic. I guess rustic meant anywhere away from my Wii. They wouldn't even let me bring my Nintendo 3DS, the jerks. Yeah, we go camping to get Dennis away from all the nasty Japanese entertainments, and then bam, he gets bitten by a werewolf. I kinda wanna say that's ironic, but I think it's more just a really bad vacation.

Like I said, I don't remember any of it, but the day we came back, I noticed these little punctures on my hand, which *could* have been bites, but I'm not sure. At the time I just thought it was from when I decided to climb the tree to show off for that hot girl two camping sites over and I fell off and I was grabbing for all these branches and stuff. Yeah, not fun. And it's not just me, 'cause Dad totally got this raging case of poison oak while we were there, so it really kinda sucked all around.

Okay, you wanna hear the most embarrassing werewolf story ever? I'm a werewolf for like two years, right? This is my life: go to school, come home, don't get dates, listen to The Cure, read Clive Barker. Very emo and seriously freakin' boring, right? The only interesting thing at all is the whole werewolf part. Only it's not really cool 'cause you can't tell anyone, thus it stops being interesting. Let me put it a better way: imagine any teenage life ever and then amplify all the over-the-top anguish and torment by like twenty. Basically, my life is a Smiths song with fur. And my only friend is Beth, who used to live next door but then she moved across town and she goes to a new school and I don't get to see her all the time anymore, so it's just me. You wanna talk lonely? Any time I hear anyone say that they're lonely, I just wanna go mental. Try being the only werewolf teenager in podunk Brock, Texas, and then we'll see how well you're defining loneliness.

Anyway, this one day my parents are away on their ski vacation they take once a year, so I decide to call Beth up. Werewolf with a house to himself, and the only thing I've done so far is watch my dad's pornos and drink a little of Mom's Santoro. Someone silver bullet me now. But Beth comes over around eight and we're watching some Japanese game show on the couch and then we just start making out. Not because we're really into each other or anything, but just because Brock is way small and there aren't exactly a whole lot of prime candidates to choose from. Mainly, though, it's 'cause Beth and I are comfortable with each other, and bored with Brock. I knew since the first time I came that Beth was gonna be the one I lost my virginity to, and it's not so much exciting as it is...

predestined, I guess. It sounds sad and a little awful when I write it out, but it's actually okay. Beth's cool.

We're making out and I go to unhook her bra, and all of a sudden my mouth is right at her neck. Right there! And it's not like I got this whole wolf-out thing going on, I mean I still pretty much felt like me. But all at once, I got this idea that if I bit her and turned her into a werewolf, I wouldn't be so alone. Can you guess the problem yet? Yeah, pretty much all I know about being a werewolf is that it really, really hurts when you start to change (imagine all your bones breaking, at once, and then like fusing themselves together at all these weird angles; *this* is the part I get to remember. My life = a big box of awesome, let me tell you right now.) I start nibbling on her neck like she likes, and then I start biting it, and Beth's all into it, grabbing my balls and stuff and squeezing them like in that one porno of my dad's that we watched, *Mean Little Bitches*. And then I *really* go to town, but, okay, I don't know what I'm doing! Is this the jugular, is that the jugular, am I even supposed to be *going* for the jugular? These are questions I need answers to. But here I am, slobbering all over Beth's neck and sort of trying to bite but not wanting to hurt her, if that makes any sense. I mean, it's *Beth*, and just 'cause I want her to be a werewolf doesn't mean I want to cause her pain. Isn't that a little insane, if you think about it? It doesn't matter, anyway, 'cause the second I start doing it harder, Beth gets all freaked and pushes me away to my side of the couch.

"The fuck are you doing," she says, buttoning up her shirt. I kinda shrugged. "No, seriously Dennis. Explain yourself or I am *so* outta here."

I decided then and there that I would have to tell her. If I didn't, she'd just think I was some creep who wanted to rape her or something and she'd probably never come over again.

"Okay, Beth, this is gonna be weird when I say it," I told her, "But you have to believe me." She looked a little sketched out, but she crossed her arms and she nodded.

"I'm a werewolf," I told her, and you have no idea how monumentally stupid that sounds out loud until you say it.

I sat there expecting one of two things. One, Beth would wig out and start punching me or something and then take off, or two, she'd laugh and laugh and point at me and laugh some more, and then take off. Not the best options, but what do you expect when you tell someone you're a lycanthrope? But Beth, always surprising, didn't do either. Instead she just looked at me.

"Wait, you're a werewolf?"

My uncle Mark is gay and he told me once that it gets easier the more you tell people. Telling people you're a werewolf is exactly the opposite of that. "Yeah," I said.

"How do you know?"

I told her about changing and how much it hurt and not remembering anything until the next morning, when I felt all tired and trench-mouthed. Beth looked at me for a real long time then, her shirt only mostly buttoned over her boobs and I was just about to ask her if she wanted to just fuck and forget the whole thing when she said she had something to tell me, too.

"What, you're a werewolf, too?" I asked her, now starting to feel my heart beating in my chest and that ball-crawling nervousness I probably shoulda felt when I told her. And she says no... and then she starts to *change*.

I'm watching her, sitting on my side of the couch, quite totally freaked out of my head. Then she stops, and I notice that her ears are bigger, and pointed. Her eyes are red now instead of blue. And, oh yeah, *Beth's got fangs!*

"Vampire," she says, and smiles.

I'm just staring at her. "You're a vampire."

"Well, the evidence suggests it, don't you think?"

"Okay, this is *so* news," I said, getting up and drinking some more Santoro right out of the bottle.

"This is not news," she said, taking the bottle from me and swigging herself. "There are vampires all over Texas. There's like eight of them right here in Brock. Now a werewolf; *that's* cool."

"I wonder if cool's the word we're looking for," I said. "And can you change back, you're weirding me out." She did and then smiled at me.

"I've been a vampire for about three years. How about you?"

"Two." Then I looked at her neck and saw where my teeth had all scratched it up. "Three years and you never tried to bite me?" I asked her. She shook her head.

"Naw, but I probably would've eventually. Don't feel bad, Dennis. Vampires are a dime a dozen, but you never see werewolves, let me tell you."

And I wanted to say, no, let me tell *you*, but I decided to leave it alone. For the first time since I got bitten I was happy, if *extremely* embarrassed. I mean, no matter if your best friend's a vampire or not, trying to bite them probably isn't the best thing in the world to do. So Beth was a vampire (ever wonder how girl vampires can put on makeup so well? I mean, with the no mirror thing, it's gotta be hard, right?) and not a werewolf, but she was still someone I could talk to, and that was a big help. She told me that after she became a vampire (it happened at this sleepover at one of her girlfriend's houses), she couldn't just leave and go to school during the day anymore, so she hid out in the basement until her mom went to work. Eventually, the school called her mom and there was this big fight, and Beth ended up turning her mom into a vampire, too. Oh, she got *totally* grounded for that one, but at least her mom doesn't try to make her go to school anymore, so there's a plus. "And homeschooling is like *so* easy," she told me. "I got an A in *French*."

We never did end up having sex that night, but by that point, it didn't even matter. Right on the spot, Beth decided that she was gonna be the go-to girl for all things werewolf. I'm a rarity, I guess, and rarities fascinate Beth. Or maybe it's actually me that fascinates her. Like I said, Brock's tiny. Just as sex will eventually be inevitable between us, I don't think we're all that immune to the love thing, either. Some days I can't tell if it's the werewolf or the guy that's she's all into, but I'd like to think it's a little bit of both. I think we're probably gonna end up together, and if that's true, I hope that it's more than my fur-n-fangs that keep her around.

For her part, she's been trying to introduce me to her world as much as she can... but it's not easy. Excepting Beth, vampires are not down with their wolven brethren. Beth even tried to take me to Jake's once, but the bouncer at the door took one look at me and asked me point-blank if I was a werewolf. (What, do I have this glowing green "W" on my forehead or something?) I said yeah and he pointed to this tiny little sign that like no one could ever see taped up near the door. NO WEREWOLVES it said. The guy elucidated: "This place is for real vamps, and the Lestat wannabes." He motioned with his hand, and I turned to see this whole huge line of goth kids who all looked like extras from *The Crow*. You know, it's kind of no fair that vampires get their own clothes and stuff, with their black clothes and pale makeup and everything. What do werewolves get? Well, judging by me, a lot of Old Navy shirts and jeans from The Gap. Then again, if I really wanted to be honest, most of those goth kids were either gonna be vamps or snacks before the end of the night, so I guess I got off pretty well.

Something else kinda cool did happen that night, though, and I guess if I'm gonna tell everything I should probably stick this in. Until Beth and I actually go at it for real, I guess what happened next will probably be the coolest thing that ever happened to me. It was the only time I ever remember what happened after I changed, which I think has to do with the fact that there wasn't a full moon.

Anyway, I'm grumbling away from Jake's and even though I told Beth to go in without me, she tagged along. We'd hitched out to Austin (both of us being all superior about not killing/eating the trucker; Beth has taken a strict "no evil" stance, very cool) and I was apparently going to walk back. Beth kept trying to lead me back toward the road, but I was like, whatever. A grumpy Dennis is not a fun Dennis. Up ahead, there was this fenced-in graveyard, way bigger than the one in Brock, and I started sprinting toward it. Creature of the night thing or just angsty teenager wanting to revel in the awfulness of it all? You decide.

I hurl myself over the fence and Beth's right behind me and I've got my hands in my jacket pockets and I'm just fuming. Because I'm stupid, I decided to blame a nearby tree for my current predicament, and I punched it. You know what happens when you punch a tree? You still have your anger, but also bloody knuckles. You also want to howl, but without a full moon, you're less Warren Zevon and more Allen Ginsberg. "I hate vampires!"

Beth came up behind me and picked up my hand gingerly and looked me in the eye. "Not me, though, right?" Whatever else you say about her, Beth has a way of deflating the rage balloon.

"Not you," I said, and smiled at her. Then she lifted my hand to her mouth and started licking the blood off my knuckles. Maybe it should have creeped me out, but it actually made me feel good. Not like horny good, just regular good. Safe, I guess.

And maybe things would have escalated to horny good if the fucking zombies didn't pick *that second* to start coming out of the ground.

It started right below me, which is probably just what I get for having my maybe-girlfriend licking my hand on top of a grave. One second, my eyes are closed and I'm having a happy, and the next, this dead hand shoots out of the earth and grabs onto my ankle.

"The fuck?" And then I'm opening my eyes and looking down.

"Oh great," Beth said, more than half-bored. "Zombies. That's just what I need in my life."

"Zombies?" I asked, trying to wriggle my foot away. Now that my eyes were all the way open, and it's happening all over the cemetery: hands plunging up out of the earth, clutching, grabbing. My only question is this: why pick *this* moment to ruin my good time? I mean, seriously. Do the forces of darkness just stand around thinking up ways to piss me off?

That's when I started, and for a second I wasn't really sure how to handle it. I mean, no full moon, I'm not in bed mentally preparing for it (how to prepare for changing into a werewolf, by Dennis Morbach: drink buttermilk, listen to Mom's Glen Campbell CD, and think naughty thoughts about Angelina Jolie. It doesn't stop the change, but it all sure puts me in a mellow place. You know, before all the bone-snapping whatnot.) Then it's like someone kicked me to the ground, because all at once I'm all hunched over with all fours on the ground. Oh, and by the way, here comes the blindingly painful bone-crunching, and fur starting to sprout everywhere... and then there's more. For the first time, I can totally feel my hands and my feet change shape, and my ears, and even the beat of my heart. And we can *finally* put to rest the notion that I change into the Lon Chaney-type werewolf with the standing upright and the hunched brow. No, when I wolf out, I go all the way. So that's something I know now.

Behind me, Beth was screaming. Well, I thought she was. When I whipped my head around, I saw she wasn't screaming: she was *laughing*. And jumping up and down and clapping, like a cheerleader or something. I also noticed that her fangs were out, and it didn't freak me out as much this time. See, *now* I was getting to horny good. Maybe it's the whole primal baser natures thing.

First though, there were zombies to take care of.

Let's get this out of the way: I had no idea how fast I was when I was a wolf. These are the times you wish Mr. Engstrom, your track coach from freshman year who kicked you off the team because you were "the slowest goddamn person I've ever met, Morbach" could see you now. First off, I wrenched out of that first zombie's grip and like *totally* took his arm off at the elbow. It went flying toward Beth and she kind of karate-chopped it away, still laughing. Beth's weird.

Then I went after all the others like it was Whack-a-Mole. They clawed out of the ground and I lunged at them, jaws clenched, claws of fury, and just ripped their heads off their decomposing necks. I've read every issue of *Walking Dead*, and I sure as hell know how to kill zombies. They tasted like shit, but I was beyond caring, because I was *aware*, you know? I was a wolf and I *knew* I was a wolf, muscular and fast and with a goddamned sense of purpose. Man, you shoulda seen those heads fly. *Jesus.*

At one point I looked up, and Beth is taking out the zombies I'm not getting by literally *ramming her high heels through their skulls*. Here I thought I was strong. She's got her head thrown back and she's laughing like crazy and it's like one of those Seger songs my mom likes to play to drive me crazy when she's cleaning the house: Beth and me, we're young and strong and probably in love, and we are having the time of our lives. I mean, we *owned* those bitches. It was all over in less than ten minutes, but while it was happening, all I can remember is being completely happy and completely *sane* for the first time in forever.

Afterward, Beth and I hung outside the gate of the cemetery, watching to make sure none of the dead folks were thinking of getting up again. I didn't really see how they *could* think, what with their dozens of heads scattered all over the place, ragged holes in like half of them, but better to be safe than sorry, right?

Eventually, Beth picked up my hand and looked at it. No more cut knuckles.

"You get healing?" she pouted. "We don't get healing!"

"Werewolf perks," I said, and I kissed her even though I had sewer-breath. Maybe I should make Altoids a part of my pre-changing ritual. The buttermilk probably doesn't help. See also: dead people's skulls. In any case, Beth didn't seem to mind the breath, which completely works to my advantage.

"What about food?" she asked me when I moved back.

"What about food?"

"Can you taste it?"

"Yeah," I said, thinking that this was a pretty damn strange conversation to have after getting kicked out of a vampire bar and vanquishing a zombie army.

"We can't. Can't taste ice cream or honey or anything anymore. Only blood."

I looked at her. "Jeez, that sucks." Then smiling, "No pun intended." She smiled at me and had this wistful look in her eyes, like she was sad and happy at once and thinking about something big she didn't want to talk about. I was going to ask her what she was thinking about, but that's when she put her head on my shoulder. We both closed our eyes and just sat like that for a little while.

We ended up grabbing a cab home, which cost everything we had between us. That was okay. On the way back, Beth fell asleep, and I brushed the hair out of her face, and for the first time loving her seemed less like a rote inevitability and more like something nice you didn't quite expect. It seemed awful that she'd never see the sun again. Maybe that was one of the things she'd been thinking about at the cemetery.

So the final tally is this: I guess that it's not altogether *horrible* to be a werewolf. There are some plusses. Vampires have that immortality thing, of which there was envy for at first... but that's probably gotta be annoying if you can't taste Twinkies, right? I'm not even annoyed that I can't get into Jake's anymore. It's the whole non-vague evil about the whole place. Not my deal.

Beth's newest crusade is finding me a werewolf club, but Google's been unhelpful. Real lycanthropes are few and far between, but I'm still young. Beth assures me that werewolves are uncommon, not rare (though sometimes I wonder if this is fact or placating. I'll go with fact, only because Beth is the only one really doing any research. I'd look into things myself, but finals are coming up, and besides, I am *so* close to unlocking the Aerosmith stuff in *Rock Band* it's not even funny. I'll find my kind sooner or later, and then the partying begins.

Till then, I've got Beth. Right now, that's just about all I need.

The Fear is in Tents

"No, seriously, he killed them all right here," Jacob said, grinning. The flashlight in his hands jittered, throwing crazy beams on the roof of the canvas tent.

"He couldn't have," Ben answered, pushing his glasses up nervously and taking another can of Pepsi from the cooler Mike's mom had packed. He wasn't scared, not him. No way. Jacob always tried to tell them these crappy stories to freak him out and they were *so* not scary, and besides, they were always made up.

"He did," Jacob shot back, nodding seriously. "It was in the papers. The Tiller Killer killed like eight girls. Maybe more. My daddy told me so."

"What's a tiller?"

Jacob rolled his eyes. "It's like this little rake you use in a garden. It has these three spikes on it and you use it to rake up dirt." He smiled. "Or *skulls*."

"So," Mike began quietly. Both Jacob and Ben turned to look at him. Mike was usually really quiet, so everyone paid attention when he spoke. "This guy, this Tiller Killer guy? He was caught?"

Jake grinned, putting the flashlight to the bottom of his face to look spooky. Ben wasn't scared of Jacob, no way. But best to close his eyes for a second, just the same.

"Nope," Jacob told them. "He was never caught. No one knows who he was or where he went to. All they found was his hand-tiller, and there were flecks of blood on every point." Jacob said this last slowly, deliberately, grinning the entire time.

All right, fine, okay, Ben was scared. But just a little.

"Bullshit," Mike said after a few moments. Ben felt relieved immediately. "No way a serial killer could have gotten away with that. I mean, this is Benny's back field. There's too many people around."

"It wasn't Benny's back field a hundred years ago, stupid," Jacob retorted, looking angry. "There was an abandoned farm up where Ben lives now—my dad says that's where the killer lived."

"But how come no one ever found him there?" Mike asked. Ben was glad to have Mike along. When he and Jacob were alone, Jake always tried to scare the crap out of Ben. Mike always made Jake's stories seem more like bullshit, and thus safer.

"Because, idiot, he hid out when the cops came around. You don't think he stuck around after killing those girls, do you?"

"Where do you get this crap, Jake?" Mike asked after a second. He was smiling, but Ben could tell Mike didn't like Jake to call him stupid or idiot. Jake smiled back, seemingly not aware that Mike's smile was fake.

"My dad tells me. He hears a lot of it down at the mill." Jake's dad, like Ben's dad and Mike's Mom, worked at the paper mill on the Marsh Hollows side of Staketon. You could still smell the stink down here clear cross town on the New Haven side.

"Well, *stupid*," Mike said, pinching his face up like Jake's did sometimes, "If he believes this stuff as much as you do, I know where you get your stupidness from." Mike smiled. Jake lunged at Mike, and for a second, Ben thought they were really going to fight. Soon, though, they were both laughing, rolling around a little.

"Come on, you guys," he said, smiling in spite of himself, "You're gonna knock my tent down."

"Hey, how come Ben gets the big tent?" Jake asked, sitting up and punching Ben playfully in the shoulder.

"Yeah, what's up with that?" Mike added, punching Ben playfully on the other shoulder.

"It's my back field," Ben said proudly, cracking them all up. The tent thing had been a great idea. All three of them still couldn't believe their parents went along with it.

"Hey, wanna hear me make an armpit fart?" Jake asked, and without waiting for an answer, stuck his hand in his shirt. In a few minutes, all three of them were trying to out-fart each other, Jake in the lead.

This was too cool.

* * *

"No, Sharon," Ben's mother said, holding the cordless and pushing the lace curtain to the side of the window over the sink, "I can still see their flashlights out there. It looks like they're all in Ben's tent."

"Oh, Cynthia, are you sure this was a good idea?" Mike's mother asked her, her voice a little tinny over the cordless. "I mean, they're only nine."

"Sharon, boys are much more mature now than they were back when we were nine. Trust me, they're f..."

"Cynthia?"

"Hold on, Sharon, I thought I heard a noise." There *had* been something, Cynthia was sure—a kind of shuffling noise out on the back porch. She peeked out the small window over the sink again, but the angle was bad and the porch was dark.

"Cyn?"

"Sharon, I'll call you right back. I think there's a stray cat or a dog or something out on the porch."

She put the phone down slowly by the side of the sink, her head cocked to the side, listening for the shuffling noise again. No noise came.

"Doesn't hurt to check though," she said to herself, grabbing the industrial size flashlight charging on the wall and crossing the kitchen to the door. She put her hand on the doorknob. It was cool. She turned it slowly, moving her head forward a little, nudging the flashlight out of the crack ahead of her.

"Hey kitty, kitty, kitty," she whispered, poking her head out. The light breeze of the August night kissed her face. She illuminated the back porch with the flashlight, crisscrossing it with the bright beam. Nothing there but the little wood porch Robert had built a few years ago, complete with flower bed holders attached to the railings.

"Must have run away," she said with a content sigh, and then something grabbed her neck from behind and hoisted her up, squeezing tight. Foul breath cascaded over her face, a stench of death, of decay, making her bile rise. Her hands clenched open and shut, trying to beat against whoever was holding her. Fear shot through her like a ricocheting bullet, blasting through her insides explosively.

"*Where's my tiller, bitch?*" the voice said, low and edgy and hollow, like tombstones grating against each other. "*They stole my tiller and I want... it... back.*"

Cynthia tried to scream, to call for Robert, but a large, fetid hand clamped over her mouth and held it shut. The other hand still clutching her neck moved closer to the front, tightening over her windpipe.

Oh please oh god oh please oh God, Cynthia's mind buzzed. Her eyes were wide, flickering everywhere, catching the sky, and the porch, and the field. The field! The boys!

"*I want my till...*" But that was all Cynthia heard, because the stars in the sky swum all together, and suddenly there was a bright flash of white, then nothing but black.

* * *

WSJS was the only damn station this side of New Haven that got any decent rock and roll. Not that new shit that Benny listened to, those "alternative" rock freaks. No, SJS got the good stuff: Springsteen, Zep, the Stones, the Beatles. All that good shit. Robert liked to listen to SJS when he worked on his projects, which was frequently. Tonight, he wanted to finish a book rack he was making for the downstairs bathroom. He hated to read, but Cyn loved it, and he was pretty sick of finding books all over the floor and the toilet. This was going to be her birthday surprise, like the chess board last year.

Besides, woodworking was a way to get his mind off of things. Right now, he didn't want to think too much.

He reached over to the bin marked *Sandpaper*. Robert Dorgan was meticulous about that, keeping everything neat and ordered. He'd had good upbringing, even if his dad did die leaving Mom with too many debts to pay, and leaving him working at the friggin' paper mill since he'd been old enough to work. Still, a lot of the upbringing stayed with him, so everything in his workspace-slash-garage came in neat little bins: *Wood Tools, Cyn's Garden Stuff, Wrenches*, et cetera. It was a way to keep your appearances neat when your inside life was a mess.

After he finished sanding down the last leg, Robert stood back and looked at his book rack. It was complete. That feeling of pride washed through him again, as it always did when he completed a project. He was damn *good* at this shit. Why couldn't he try to make a living out of this?

His smile faltered. Best not to live in dreams. He was living on borrowed time, anyway. No use in thinking crazy shit like that anyway. Best to just stain the rack and get up to bed. It had been a long day.

As he reached for the can of stain underneath his work bench, Robert Dorgan thought he heard something behind him. He stood, turned, and saw nothing but the Jeep and a lot of shadow.

"Calm yourself down, Bobby," he whispered quietly, "It doesn't mean anything. Nothing's going to happen." But suddenly, it seemed best to save the staining until morning. Bed was sounding pretty good right now.

His fingers touched the toggle switch next to his work station. All of a sudden, Robert didn't want to turn it off. Anything could happen in the dark, and it was about five feet to the door that led into the house. Screw the light, he thought. Who cares if the electric bill runs a little high this month?

Robert took his hand off the switch, turned to walk in front of the Jeep, when something sharp rammed through his left hand and deep into the wood work bench. Pain shot up through his arm and Robert screamed. He looked down and saw an awl jutting from the top of his hand, a few inches below his middle knuckle. Blood squirted like errant water from a hose with pinpricks in it. He looked back, looked behind him, and one of the shadows came forward.

"*Tiller*," the voice coming from the shadow uttered. It was the voice of graves, of death.

"No, please no!" Robert yelled, trying to loosen his hand from the work bench. The shadow moved forth, and Robert could smell the stench emanating from it, a sickly black-yellow odor of rot and madness. A hand came into the light, yellow and putrid. Worms burrowed into the soft, coalescent flesh there. Robert felt his gorge rise. He wet his pants. The radio above the workstation played "Domino," by Van Morrison.

The hand reached up, gently touching the bins Robert had labeled so neatly. It lay its bony finger on the first bin, *Sandpaper*, the second bin, *Wood Tools*, stopping at the third bin, *Cyn's Gardening Stuff*. It reached in. Robert could hear the sounds of metal being rummaged through. A moment later, the movement stopped.

"My tiller!" that dead, lunatic voice cried trium-
phantly. Robert saw it was indeed Cynthia's tiller, its
three curved spikes gleaming. The thing moved forward, holding the tiller high. Robert thought of the
boys in the back field, wanted to scream *Run! Run!* but
he knew they wouldn't hear him. Instead, he thought
of his own childhood, and the two friends he had had,
much like Robert's son and his two friends. And while
he thought that, the tiller came down on his right
cheek, burying itself there. Robert screamed again.
The owner of the voice, the shadow, dragged the tiller
across Robert's face, ripping the skin to shreds, rending the muscle from bone. Blood erupted everywhere,
spattering the bench, his newly made book rack, and
the tiny, tinny radio above. Van Morrison didn't seem
to mind. SJS was in the middle of a triple-shot of Van,
and boy, could that Irish boy rock.

Robert died convulsing in a pool of his own blood,
thinking of Florida.

* * *

"Ben?" Mike said from his own tent a foot away.
"Ben? You asleep?"

"Not really," Ben whispered back, turning to his
side and turning the flashlight on. "It's sort of hard to
sleep on the ground."

"No shit," Jake said from farther away. Ben smiled
a little. Jake used swear words like he didn't even
care. Usually when he and Mike said something bad
they started laughing. Like they had been caught, or
something. Not Jake. He just came right out and said
it, no problem.

"Ben, can I come into your tent?" Mike asked, a
little nervously. Jake laughed a little.

"Benny? Can I come into your tent-y?" Jake
mocked. "It's scaaaary out here alone." Jake laughed
again. Mike spoke up.

"It *is* scary out here... dickhead." Ben covered his mouth so Jake wouldn't hear him laugh.

"Okay, you win," Jake said, his voice coming closer. "It *is* scary out here. We're coming over, Ben."

When they all got settled in Ben's larger tent, Mike said, "I thought I heard something moving out there."

"You're just scared at that story I told you, Mike," Jake said, but this time, his tone wasn't mocking. He seemed a little scared himself.

"Yeah," Ben said, shifting nervously in his sleeping bag. "It was probably just a cat or something."

"No, guys, really," Mike said, and something in his face made Ben believe him. He seemed too sure, too scared. Mike was *never* scared.

"Don't worry about it, Mikey," Jacob said. "If the Tiller Killer comes back, we'll just feed Ben to him and get away."

"Bite me," Ben said, laughing a little, and Jake was about to move over to do just that when they all heard the noise—the sound of nylon tearing open. And it was close.

The boys froze. Ben was bathed in sweat. They heard the noise again.

Rrrrrrriiiiippppppp. Rrrrrrrriiiiiiiiiiiiiippppppppp.

Someone's tearing one of the tents up, Ben thought. Then, they heard the voice carrying over to them from a few feet away. From where Ben was sure the ruins of Jake's tent was.

The voice, like bones grinding, said *"Tiller."*

The boys screamed in unison, leaping up, scrambling to get out of the tent. Ben dropped his flashlight and it fell to the ground, the light blowing out. The front of Ben's tent faced away from Jake's, so their backs were turned from whatever spoke in that hideous, ugly voice.

They ran toward the house. Ben, in the rear, didn't look behind him. He wanted to, wanted to see, but he forced himself not to. If he saw, he might stop. And if he stopped, it might get him. Because it was following them, oh yes, it was coming close. Ben could smell it, like a moving swamp.

Jake reached the house first, near the back porch where they'd stored their bikes earlier that day.

"Get on your bikes!" Jake yelled, "We'll go to my house!"

Jake found his, a blue Huffy, and jumped on it, pedaling away. Ben saw Mike grab his and run with it toward the street, which was lightly traveled at five and deserted by eight. No one was around. No one could help them. Ben grabbed his bike, then looked up at the porch. There was a shape there, lying half in the doorway, half out. It looked familiar. Ben stopped, frozen. Should he put his bike down, should he go see? That shape... it couldn't be what he thought it was, no way, but...

"*Tiller*," the voice croaked from behind, and now it was *very* close.

Ben's paralysis broke. He leapt on his bike and began pedaling furiously, sweat standing out on his forehead, cool in the night. Behind him, he heard a small *clink*, metal against metal, and he could smell that putrid odor reaching out, trying to envelop him. He screamed, a high, reedy scream that echoed in the night.

Ten minutes later, he found Mike and Jake pounding at Jake's door.

"Mommy!" Jake yelled, "Let us in!" Ben ran up the brick steps and began pounding with them. A moment later, the front light came on, and Mrs. Wilson opened the door.

"Jakie?" she asked, more confused than concerned. "Honey, what's wrong? I thought you were staying in Benny's back field."

"Mom! There's somebody after us, somebody... dead!" Mike and Ben nodded. Ben found himself unable to speak.

"Oh, boys," Mrs. Wilson said, rubbing her eyes. "You were probably telling ghost stories, and..." She stopped short. Ben saw her eyes widen, staring down at the bottom of the brick steps. They turned, and all of them saw.

Attached to the small reflector dish on the back of Ben's bike was a hand-tiller, dripping blood from each of its points. The bony, yellow hand was still gripping the handle.

Busting Heavies

I have been in the cage only a day and a half and already Walsh has brought a new victim. He struggles heroically, screaming and bucking. Hectic, panicky color screams from his cheeks and forehead, and sweat runs off of him in thick rivers. His wrists are handcuffed together in front of him. He is a fat man, like me. By my own rough estimation, the man is not quite six feet and weighs at least three hundred, maybe three hundred and twenty five pounds. Perhaps it's the weight that makes him heave in his breath like that between screams. Or perhaps it is Walsh, yanking the choke-rope hard and making the heavy man come forward out of necessity.

My cage—I fear that after less than two days I have begun to think of this prison in the possessive—stands in the corner of a sparsely decorated basement room. The cage is bolted to the wall and the bars are quite thick. In its own odd way, my prison reminds me of church, not that I've ever been much of a religious man. Inside, there are only three choices: sit, stand, and kneel. I suppose if I were thinner I'd be able to curl into a ball if I needed to sleep. As of yet, though, I haven't felt the desire to sleep much. This situation has me too keyed up.

Across from my cage stands a large plywood table, with twin semicircles of iron set into the wood at each corner. As Walsh forces the other man toward the table, I see that these are rudimentary cuffs, and that the table as a whole comprises a horizontal stocks. I grasp the bars of the cage and watch with wide eyes as the man screams for me to help him, but I can't help. I wish I could.

Walsh reaches behind his back with one hand, holding the slip-knotted rope in the other, and lifts up the back of his shirt. Even from my decidedly compromised viewpoint, I see what he has tucked there: it is a handgun. I am not proficient enough in handgun knowledge to be able to discern the make and model, but I see it is a black pistol with a snubnose. Walsh brings it out and touches it against the heavy man's red, sweaty forehead. He orders the man to lie down on the table. The man complies. Like me two days before, this man seems to have run out of options.

Tucking the pistol into the front of his pants, but still keeping a grip on the choke-rope, Walsh secures the man's ankles into the leg-cuffs. Then he moves around to the head of the table and stretches the man's left arm and secures that, too. Now, the fat man is wailing, a loud, desultory sound that reverberates off the walls of the basement room. Walsh mutters something about soundproofing and closes the final cuff around the big man's right wrist. Now we are both locked up.

Walsh turns to me now, and again the shivers wrack my body. He smiles, but there is no joy in that smile. I try to glimpse some humanity in his pale blue eyes, but I see none. Not for the first time these past few days I begin to wonder about the nature of pure evil. Could it be here, standing in front of me? Could it be smiling?

In a voice just above a whisper, Walsh tells me to wait for the show. He is nearly inaudible above the high, desperate shrieking going on behind him. I want to ask him what he means. What show? But my throat locks, and I am unable to speak. Maybe it is the abject terror which courses through my large body like an electrical current. Or maybe it is because I haven't had anything to drink in nearly ten hours.

Walsh exits through a door on the far wall, and returns five minutes later with three items: a Shop-

Vac, a butcher knife, and a pair of scissors. The metal blades should terrify me, and they do, but for some reason it's the vacuum that makes my skin crawl coldly across my bones. Suddenly, I feel like screaming in unison with the man on the table, but something inside me tells me that Walsh will leave me alone if I'm quiet.

Sweat pours off of me as Walsh brings his implements closer. The sound of the vacuum's wheels against the cold stone floor is lonely and hollow. Walsh's face remains calm, as usual, and his eyes are granite flecks set in canyon sockets. Now, his head turns away from me, his attention aimed solely at the fat man on the table. For a moment, the man's screaming had stopped; now, as Walsh moves the scissors to the man's stomach, the man begins to shriek. The sound bites through the stale air in the basement like teeth through soggy bread.

Walsh grabs the bottom of the man's shirt, a cotton Polo shirt with a little horse-and-rider insignia on the lapel, lifts it, and begins cutting into it with the scissors. Soon, the man's belly is exposed, a large white expanse of skin and stretch marks. His navel is cavernous. As Walsh slices the top part of the shirt off, the man's hairless chest sags; he's got a set of man-tits on him, and they loll to each side. Absurdly, an odd species of shame pummels me, the shame of the fat man not comfortable with his body. The shame of knowing you haven't skipped a meal in a long time, and the shame of knowing that you wore size thirty-six pants only seven or eight years ago. This shame tastes bitter, especially in the center of this horror show.

Walsh hums absently, a tune that doesn't follow a rhythm or melody. He doesn't speak. Instead, he raises one large hand up and brings it down forcefully, slapping the man in the stomach as hard as possible. The shrieks stop, and now the man is reduced to sobbing. It hurts to hear that sound in a place like this. It's the sound of capture without release. It's the sound of desperation.

The scissors are placed on a small bench near the table. Now, Walsh reaches for the butcher knife. Gently, he touches the tip to the man's enormous stomach, trailing it lightly across the surface. The man's blubbering intensifies. Blood seeps from the shallow cut-line Walsh is drawing in the belly. For a moment, Walsh pauses, closing his eyes and muttering something even I can't hear. Then, without warning, he drives the knife into the belly and the screaming resumes.

I avert my eyes. I don't want to watch, to see Walsh slicing this man to pieces. I am crying now, I know. I can't help myself. What's happening is too horrible to handle, too upsetting. And yet I find my eyes shifting back to look. To see. It's too horrible to look but I find I must. And that action, I fear, is what damns me.

Walsh has not begun to slice the man in parts, as I had guessed. Instead, he is intently sawing into the large stomach, his brow a furrow of concentration. Just as listlessly as the blood had seeped from the shallow cut, it now spouts from the hole Walsh is cutting. That's what it is, I see: a hole. The movement of the knife is definitely circular, the blood gushing from the wound like that of water from an irregularly shaped hose. In my shock and disgust, I scream. Even though I fear for myself, I am unable to stop. The natural reaction centers of my brain have overridden the logic circuits, and I am no longer in control of my motor functions.

The vacuum whirrs to life by Walsh's feet, and I assume that he has kicked the ON switch. Blood spatters his face in a gush, but he doesn't seem to mind. That cold, expressionless look never leaves his eyes, even as he blinks away drops of blood. Even over the whirring sound of the vacuum, I can hear him whispering. He is telling the man to get thin, get thin. He raises the nozzle of the vacuum to the screaming man's stomach, and just as I realize what Walsh is going to do, I vomit. My last meal was nearly two days ago, but still I vomit, and when I can no longer vomit, I begin to dry heave. And I cannot tear my eyes away. God help me, I cannot tear my eyes away.

Walsh begins to insert the vacuum into the hole he has created in the man's stomach, but the fit is imperfect and he has to grind the nozzle in. Suddenly, the whir of the vacuum becomes less reedy and more a low grinding. The sound of the man's blood splattering into the wet/dry reservoir soon supersedes the sound of the motor, brings the horror to the forefront. I dry heave again.

Suddenly, the motor sound becomes insistent, panicky. I have lived alone for five years and I understand what that sound means: the vacuum is stuck on something it can't suck up. Walsh seems to understand this. Swiftly, he plucks the nozzle from the man's stomach. The man's screams have reached a fever pitch, and I wonder how long he can go on screaming like that. Walsh reaches toward the bench, grabs the butcher knife, and jabs it into the spouting hole. This time, instead of cutting downward, he seems to be slicing vertically, and I realize with a sick dread what he is doing. The vacuum had caught on another organ, or the wall of the man's stomach. Maybe his spleen. Walsh is shredding the obstruction so it, too, can be sucked up easily. When he eventually jams the vacuum back into the hole, the sound of splattering is accompanied by a meatier sound, the sound of sliced-up organs propelled into a pool of blood. I wonder if any of this can really be happening, if I can really be seeing what I am seeing, and my mind whispers back, yes, yes I can, and I believe it. I believe it because I can see the blood, and smell the shredded guts as they enter the vacuum's bowels, and hear the sound of the vacuum at work, and the unsettling sound of the man's screams diminishing. I can taste my tears on my lips and feel the cold sweat standing out on my forehead.

I believe this is happening because my senses dictate that I believe it, but my inner heart wants to turn away and say no, this cannot be in a sane world.

But now I know the secret. This is not a sane world.

* * *

An unfathomable time later, the man is dead, his screams closed off forever. Walsh's vacuum is full, as the hideously deflated body on the table leads me to assume. I am still crying, but my gorge is safely low. I no longer feel the need to vomit.

I simply stand in my cage in the corner of the room, gripping the iron bars and staring at the body and wondering if it is possible to get used to depravity. Throughout the entire ordeal, Walsh remained expressionless, stolid. Has he killed before? If so, is he numb to killing now? Now the larger questions come to mind. Why big men? As far as I know, the only two victims Walsh has chosen are me and the recently deceased man on the table. Both of us are—or, in the case of the other man, *were*—decidedly overweight. Fat, to be honest. Both of us are fat. Which leads to the biggest question at the moment: Why did Walsh kill the other man immediately and not kill me?

Now, though, the questions disappear as Walsh returns with a long cardboard box. The word BALL is stenciled in green across the white front, above the illustration of a glass jar. Walsh places the box gently on the floor, removes a jar, and unscrews the top. Gently, he places the nozzle into the Ball jar, and kicks a switch on the side of the vacuum. I assume it is the "reverse" button. Reddish chunks of sodden organs splatter against the inside of the glass, blood surging in to coat them like marinara sauce. My stom-ach turns queasily as I see that some of the blood has clotted and small circles of black-brown clot float in the nearly full jar. When one jar is full, Walsh repeats the process. After eight or nine Ball jars have been filled, Walsh returns to his work bench and produces a heavy black marker and a sheet of labels. He turns slightly to the table the body is still lying on and puts the sheet down. I see that the labels are bordered with a thin green vine print; these labels were designed for the outside of fruit jars. But Walsh does not write *fruit* on his labels. He writes *VISCERA*.

* * *

Days have passed. I am still in this cage, this god-damn cage, and I think the walls are beginning to move in on me. The darkness is tangible. I am alone and afraid and going out of my mind. When Walsh comes down, he turns on the lights and I can see out into the room, I can see the door leading into the house. But I can't get there. I used to use the phrase *everything else* a lot. Well, Jeff, I'd tell myself, finish this report and *everything else* can fall by the wayside. I can have one of everything at the buffet, I'd think to myself, those wheels of guilt turning, and then two of *everything else*. I never realized what power that phrase held. I am in this cage, this tiny iron cage and *everything else* is outside of it. That thought makes me want to cry.

Walsh hasn't murdered again, and for that I am grateful. When I finally slept, hours after Walsh had cleared the body away and put the jars of *viscera* into the small refrigerator on the far wall, I began to have nightmares. In them, the man on the table is scream-ing, but it's not the incoherent otherworldly shriek he had projected in the real world. In the space of dreams, the man is screaming my name, blaming me. In my dreams, I am at fault. I don't know why.

Since the murder, I have kept myself busy in two ways. The first is, of course, trying to figure out a way out of the cage. It is secured to the wall by two bolts welded into the first and last bars at the back of the cage. These bolts are set into a thick panel of plywood nailed to the surface of the wall, which I assume is soundproofed. If I had more leverage, I might be able to shake the cage enough to unsecure the bolts. The bolts look strong, but the raised plywood square they are fastened to does not. I keep thinking that if only I knew that Walsh was out of the house, I could throw myself against the front of the cage, and eventually tear the bolts loose from the wall.

But then I face reality again. Even if I release the cage from the wall, what would I do then? Lie on the floor, the cage still surrounding me, and wait for Walsh to come back and put me in little jars.

Besides, he hasn't been away for very long. He comes down here regularly and feeds me and gives me water. When I was first brought here, Walsh didn't feed or water me for nearly a day. When he killed the other man, I assumed his objective was to kill me, too, but slowly, by starvation or by thirst. Now, I am unsure what to think.

After shooting the inside of the fat man into jars, he hacked up the rest of him with a double-bladed ax and put those pieces in a two-ply twenty-gallon garbage bag. That bag went into three more bags and then Walsh left with it. I don't know what he did with it. Hours later, he returned with a meal for me. I couldn't help but wonder if it was the other man, cooked and served on a cardboard tray. Instead, it was a TV dinner, tasting so rubbery I knew at once that it was not real meat. I have felt no ill side effects from it. I have to assume that the food Walsh gives me is safe. I just wonder why he does it.

Why kill one fat man and leave the other alive? Why capture fat men in the first place? Why put their insides into jars and save them? I ask why and I don't understand, don't comprehend. It's too much. There is no normalcy. I am left in the dark alone and not even sleep brings me solace. In this darkness, I wish I was dead.

* * *

It is dark in here and I am roused out of sleep and nightmares. There is a noise in the blackness outside the iron bars, a noise in the room that surrounds me. In this darkness, my senses are sharper, and I can hear the low, reedy sound of breathing from somewhere at the far wall. And whispering, I hear. It is Walsh. Get thin, get thin. It is almost a chant.

I listen for a few minutes. The whispering is becoming maddening. It is quiet, and low, a long stream of nonsensical uttering. I wish he would stop. In the dark, I believe such sounds can drive a man mad. Stop. Stop. Stop.

I must have said that last aloud, for it does stop. I hear footsteps, heavy boots against the stone floor. It is Walsh. I can sense him crouching down in front of my cage, in front of the bars that hold me prisoner.

He whispers to me now. He says he hopes he didn't wake me. I don't answer. He says he knows I'm awake, the sound of my breathing is different. I admit that I am. Then, without provocation, he asks if I want to know why he does it. Why does he capture and kill fat men? Against my will, I ask him why. I need to know. The wondering has been maddening. When he answers, the voice is calm, pleased. It is not complex. He tells me he does it because he hates fat men. That they symbolize everything that is greedy and slovenly and wrong with the world. First, they must get thin. Then, they must be eradicated. Then he stops, pauses, and I hear a smile in his voice. And, he adds, because he can. It's so easy to do.

I sit in my position for a moment, sweat surging over my body. I think I may have urinated, but I can't be sure. He begins to turn away, when I ask him why me. Why am I here? What role do I serve? My mouth is acting on its own volition. I couldn't stop it if I tried.

I hear the boots turn back. Now, I hear a resigned sort of sadness in his voice. Walsh says it's because he wants me to know that this is my fault. If I hadn't gotten so fat, if these other men hadn't gotten so fat, he wouldn't have to do this. I am the symbol, the caged symbol, of his greatest hatred. I serve as a reminder to Walsh what his duty is.

Also, he says, he needs an audience.

He walks away from the cage and flicks on the light to the basement room. I am momentarily blinded, pain shooting through my head. Then I see the table. From my angle, I can only see the underside. I see the blood dripping from it. Slowly, I stand and I see that there is another man on the table. Walsh has cut a long slit down the man's gigantic belly and opened it up. A medium-size garden trowel juts out of the man's stomach, and by the proliferation of Ball jars on Walsh's work bench, I can only assume he's using the trowel to scoop out the man's insides. In addition, there is a long, sharp instrument sticking out of the man's neck, what looks like an awl.

He wanted to sever the man's larynx, Walsh explains to me as he returns to his scooping, so he wouldn't wake me up.

Now I am awake, and screaming into the madness that plays itself so calmly in front of me. Is insanity infectious? I close my eyes, still screaming, and refuse to think about the question any further. I don't want to know the answer.

* * *

Why wait until Walsh is away? The room is sound-proofed.

Ignoring the logic I argued with a day or two ago, I begin to throw myself against the bars that compose the front of the cage. I stop an hour or so later when I hear the key moving in the lock. I will bruise, I'm sure, but I am still wearing the shirt and pants I wore when I was brought here. Walsh won't see my bruises. He won't know. I pray he won't know.

* * *

I can only guess at time, but I assume a week has passed. I must only consult my internal clock, my general feelings of awake and tired. A week, and every day I get more and more terrified, more and more claustrophobic, and I fear, I fear, more and more crazy.

In this arbitrary "week," Walsh has slaughtered three more men. All fat men. I stand, watching, unable to move, unable to turn away. I realized with some trepidation after the first of these new kills that I hadn't vomited. After the second, I realized I had not screamed. I only watch, stare, as Walsh calmly sucks their guts out through the Shop-Vac and redeposits them into Ball jars. As he hacks them to little pieces and stuffs those into garbage bags. I watch, I stare, and I become more and more used to the horror.

Sometimes after he slaughters the men he brings, Walsh stands in front of my cage. Over and over again, he tells me it is my fault. I must be assigned the blame. As long as I am alive as a symbol of how men destroy their bodies, then more must die. He says it calmly, as if reciting a litany of facts. There is no debate. When I look in his eyes as he recites this diatribe, I see a thin blank nothing. There is no sense of purpose in him, no sense of glee or sadness or importance. All I see is nothing, and I sit in the darkness in my cell and wonder if it is insanity I am looking into or the personification of evil.

I must escape.

Dear God, I must escape.

* * *

The light flicks on. At once, I stop throwing myself against the front of the cage. Immediately I know something is wrong. Walsh bullets through the door grasping the choke-rope. On the other end of the rope is a man, roughly four hundred pounds, but he is not screaming. And Walsh does not appear to be calm and composed. For the first time, I think he is terrified.

The heavy man is gasping, red in the face. Putting himself at risk, Walsh grabs the man's meaty hand and pulls him toward the table. The man stumbles forward, his face red, his breathing shallow. I realize what is happening: the big man is having a heart attack.

Walsh, whose muscular body writhes in polar opposite to the heavy man's, hoists the other man onto the table and locks the hand- and leg-cuffs together lightning-fast. I stare at the man on the table and feel a sad pity for him. He bucks on the table, his eyes wide and glazed. Gurgling, choking sounds erupt from his mouth. He bucks once, twice, three times against his bounds and then he lies still. His large chest falls slightly. His right hand, which has been clutching feverishly at the air, now falls open, limp. The big man is dead.

Walsh returns only moments later with the knife, the vacuum, and the scissors. There is a wild, desperate look in his eyes I have never seen before. Fresh terror awakens inside of me. When he sees the body, he stops, and only looks at it for a moment. Then, he drops his implements and rushes at the body, screaming in mad fury.

I watch, shocked, as Walsh leaps onto the table, straddles the body, and begins to pound on the chest. He is screaming that it's not fair, that this is not God's work, that this is *his* work, that he must be allowed to do this himself. Loud, wracking sobs burst from him as he screams that he does not need intervention, he is doing fine all by himself, he is saving the world from all the fat men. Now, his screams become incoherent shrieks, crazy non-sounds that pierce my eardrums and make my brain throb. Walsh stops pounding his fist on the chest and begins on the face. There is a hollow squashing sound followed by a sharp cracking of bone. And again. And again.

I am hyperventilating. There is a fundamentally evil man on top of a dead body in front of me, and he is pounding the body's face into a bloody pulp. The screams, oh dear God the screams are carrying me higher. My quick, shallow breaths give way to a long, hard inhalation, and I know I am going to begin to scream, too. I am going to echo Walsh in his madness.

Except I don't.

Except I start laughing.

* * *

No more food. It's been a day, I suppose, and there hasn't been any food. A few hours ago, I took off my shirt and wrung the sweat out of it to drink. For a smaller man, the effort would have been pointless. I wear a 2XL T-shirt. I drank enough.

The body of the heart-attack victim is still lying there. I stare at it, with its gigantic size and demolished face, and try to understand something, anything, about what is happening here. Why I feel suddenly dirty. Why my mind hurts when I look at the dead body, decaying in front of me. Why I smile thinking of Walsh in the same position.

The reason why I can stare at the body is because Walsh has gotten sloppy. He broke his own rules. The light remains on, the body remains mainly whole on the table. The door is closed, though, and that actually works in my favor. With the door open, I wouldn't have even tried to move the cage. But Walsh slammed the door when he left hours ago, and I have been bashing myself against the front of the cage ever since. I don't know if it's doing much good. The bolts don't seem to be moving at all. But I must have hope, I must, to keep the encroaching claustrophobia at bay, to keep the madness away, to keep the thought of the dead man on the table not five feet from me out of my head.

I bash myself against the iron bars and I think of Walsh bashing his fist into the dead man's face.

I bash myself against the cold iron bars and I think of Walsh screaming that it isn't fair, that he should be the one who decides whether fat men live or die.

I begin to bash myself against the bars once more, but then the door swings open and it is Walsh.

He's carrying a blowtorch. That calm, metered look is back in his eyes. I wonder if he's going to torch the body instead of just hacking it up, as punishment for not dying on his terms.

But Walsh doesn't head for the table.

He heads for me.

Slowly, he advances. He's talking, but except for his usual mantra of get thin, get thin, they seem like nonsense words. He says something about retribution. An eye for an eye. A fatty for a fatty. The torch goes on with a quiet *floomph* sound and still my captor approaches.

I begin to scream.

He reaches my cage, holds the torch out. The heat is intense. I push myself as far back to the wall as I can, which is not much. Walsh comes closer, moves the torch toward my belly, my large belly. And suddenly, something inside me snaps. I think of myself holding the torch on him. I think of my big body sitting on top of him, pounding his face in. I think of myself as evil for the first time, catching his evil and turning it around on him. The feeling is liberating. Endorphins rage through my brain. I am God.

I lurch forward, feeling the torch sear my skin, but right now it does not hurt. My sweat-drenched shirt lies on the floor of my cage and I am lucky for that; it would have surely caught fire. Fueled by adrenaline, I reach over the fire, over the torch, and through the bars to Walsh's wrist. I secure a hand around it and he drops the torch. It lands on the cement ground and the flame goes out. I am staring at Walsh with steely, calm eyes. My grip is secure. I yank him forward, bashing him against the cage. His head makes contact. He screams as he had done on top of the dead body, so I yank him forward again. I feel nothing but calm. Walsh screams again, but the screams are weaker. I yank again, and Walsh crumples to the floor.

Without thinking, I throw my entire weight to the front of the cage. I feel some slight give behind me, but not much. Again, using my full three-hundred-and-forty pounds. The cage now moves more, a slight bit. Again. Again. Again. My shoulder is bloody, my side is aching. I feel I have bruised or perhaps broken a rib. I don't care. I am God. Again. Again, and then, all at once, the cage begins to topple. Instinctively, I reach backward, grabbing the bars behind me, and as the cage falls to the floor I am saved from injury. I glance at the bolts which had held me in this prison for over a week. They are still secure. The raised block of plywood was the weakness, and the nails that held it in place. I ripped it off of the wall that last time. There are ragged holes in the wall where it used to be secured.

My energy is dissipating. I must move swiftly. I think, I hope,that the fall has broken the lock. Please God, please let the lock be broken. I thrust my weight to the side, and now it is far easier to turn the cage to its side than it was to yank it from the wall. The door of my prison is now on my right. I push on it. It doesn't budge.

Again, I feel my mind about to give. This time, however, I feel it is about to crumple like Walsh had done when I bashed his head against the bars. I feel I am sliding into the depths of myself, finally giving in to the pain and horror here, finally submitting to Walsh's madness.

But now...

Oh yes. Oh, thank God yes.

The blowtorch is still in one piece, lying near Walsh's booted feet. Tears standing out in my eyes, I reach for it, my fingers brushing lightly against the curved surface. For a moment, I feel it is just slightly out of my reach, just enough to drive me utterly, un-flinchingly mad.

But then the friction catches, and I drag the blow-torch toward me. I smile. I am God now. It feels good.

* * *

I have been in the cage for over a week but now I am out and Walsh is on the table.

He wants to scream, I see, but I have the power now, I am the fat man in power, and Walsh cannot scream. He has the vacuum cleaner nozzle shoved too far down his throat.

The dead body lies on the floor beside the table. I pushed it off and when it landed it made a splat-ting sound. Mostly-empty Ball jars are strewn around the body, each with a jarring label reading VISCERA across it. I dumped their contents into the shop vac-uum after I made sure Walsh couldn't move from the table.

Walsh looks at me, wide-eyed and staring, and for a brief moment, I wonder if I, too, am evil. Maybe such answers are beyond me.

I whisper, "Get fat."
And I flick on the vacuum's reverse.

Last Night at the Bear

"Kev! Kev!" Wade yelled after me as I stepped through the doorway and left the Happy Bear Donut Shop for the night. It was raining that night—not heavy yet, but you could tell it was going to get that way. I looked up at the sky and saw the giant, rusty Happy Bear sitting on the roof—an orange-yellow bear-thing made of painted metal. If that wasn't enough to make you puke, the smell of the deep-fried donuts could push you over the edge.

Wade came running to the door to meet me. My sigh of relief turned into a sigh of regret. Wade was going to ask me for another ride home. Wasn't that a pisser? After eight solid hours of customer whining, and cleaning up toilets, and smelling the barf-inducing frying dough, now I had to put up with Wade for another twenty minutes. Great.

And it wasn't a question of not taking him, either. That's probably what pissed me off the most. When he asked, I felt like I had to take him home. Like I didn't have a choice. Maybe I saw a little of myself in him, Wade being eighteen and living in the poor part of Sheldon. I grew up in that area because my mom, God love her, refused to get a job after Dad left and we basically lived hand to mouth on food stamps. Don't get me wrong—I think food stamps are great for people who really need it. But my mom wasn't one of the ones who really needed it—and I swore when I was ten that when I lived on my own, I would never turn to that. I'd starve before that.

Which, of course, led to my living in Maverick House, a rooming house near the edge of town that was really the only affordable place for someone living alone and working at The Bear. They always smell like Ramen noodles, which you can pick up at the Stop & Shop on Sparrow Street at the cost of twelve for a buck. When I saw Wade come into the Bear for his shift, with his thrift-store clothes and greasy, uncut hair, I knew he had spent many a mealtime chomping down those Ramen noodles—and maybe drinking some Stop & Shop generic soda, which was usually forty cents cheaper than the brand names.

"Kev! Can I get a ride?" I knew it. If I wasn't so tired, maybe I would have known something was wrong right then. Wade seemed too animated, too keyed up that night. His eyes seemed a little wild, far removed from their normal dazed complacency. Usually, it was, Wade, can you clean all the bathrooms tonight? Sure, yeah, and he'd walk off and do them, slumping. It was a pretty good thing Wade worked mostly in the back—customer service wasn't his forté, and his looks and demeanor would probably scare a few of the customers away. I've met a lot of seriously depressed people in my life (mostly in my junior year of high school—that's when the "black-clothes-and-The-Cure" phase sets in), but none so much as Wade. He walked through the day in kind of a dirge—not really speaking, not moving around unless he had to. Tina, our boss, kept him near the deep fryers most of the day, and Wade didn't really seem to mind. You sometimes wonder if a guy like that ever had dreams, and if so, how they had been obliterated so early.

I'm not saying I was much different. I'd lived in Maverick House for two years at that point. It's a transient place, full of transient men. Most of the men who lived there were old and used up and went there to die. Sometimes they were guys who had just gotten out of jail or a halfway house, and Maverick was their way to acclimate back into society. Once or twice, it was a guy whose wife had left him because he was a drunk, and he came to Maverick House to get dry in the hopes that she'd take him back. Oh yeah. By twenty, I'd shared a roof with some pretty desperate characters... although none so desperate as the fellow whose room I had moved into. You see, I got what is affectionately known at Maverick House as the Murder Room. Nice ring, don't you think?

I got the story from the girls I worked with at the Bear—mostly in their early teens and still going to Sheldon High. I checked up on it at the Sheldon Town Library, and it's all true. A man named Winston O'Brien lived in my room. Used my closet. Put his clothes in the same dresser I got the day I'd laid down my first week's rent. He also killed someone in that room, another tenant, supposedly over a dispute about whose milk was whose in the community refrigerator. It gets worse: O'Brien not only *killed* the guy, but he also *ate* him, too. At least part of him. Oh yeah. I could have inherited my room from some old guy who kicked off peacefully in the night, or some recovering junkie trying to go straight, or some other young unfortunate like myself just trying to get along. Nope. I get the cannibal murderer. Sometimes at night, I'd lie awake and wonder if that thought should bother me more than it did. I stayed up late on those nights, watching bad Elvis movies on TNT and playing solitaire chess, until I pretty much fainted from exhaustion. Maybe it was better not to think of those things at night.

Now I said, "Sure, Wade, hop in." Rain poured down from his greasy black hair in rivers. His huge Army jacket (which probably cost him ten dollars at the thrift store on Lark Avenue) hung from him limply, enveloping him in the wet. His little dark eyes twitched in his doughy face, like small marbles having seizures. Wade was never going to win for Mr. Universe, that was sure, and in that second I felt really bad for him. He wasn't conventionally ugly, but he was probably never going to find a girl who would fall in love with him at first sight. He would end up with a wife who was willing to settle, and he would probably end up coming home from his days at the Bear to a rented trailer and a black and white TV. That sounds just horrible, doesn't it? I had Wade's whole life mapped out for him because he was fat, pimply, and maybe ate Ramen noodles for dinner. But I'd seen it with my high school friends, and I thought I was seeing it with Wade—guys who start off in a life designed to drag them down, and who discover that complacency is easier than trying for better.

What was I doing at The Bear, then? Easy. I got kicked out of my house when I was Wade's age. Eighteen. I no longer qualified for government assistance under my mom's care, so I got the boot. I wasn't entirely surprised, although when it came, it hurt like hell. There was a week's time between the moment my mom said I should leave until I was spending my night in the bedroom of a murderer. Cheery thoughts, huh? It's a wonder that I got any sleep that first year at Maverick.

The big thing with me was, I was standing around judging my friends and Wade, projecting their empty futures, and not bothering to look at my own. My argument was that they all still lived with Mom or Dad, and I was able to make it on my own. I had brought myself up from the trauma of having my mom kick me out right after high school and I supported myself. But when it came right down to it, I was jealous. None of them had to worry about rent payments, or whether their food was still going to be there the next day after you just went food shopping. Maybe there was something to Winston O'Brien's dispute over milk. That first year at Maverick, I learned a lot. Keep your food in your room, keep your money hidden in a box in your dresser, and keep a lock on your door. In other words, don't trust anyone.

Wade got into my Impala and slammed the door shut. He began jittering, his head jerking around just like his eyes were. *Great,* I thought. *He's on drugs. I should have known. Why did I let him into my car?*

"Wade, you okay?" I asked, even then a little concerned. Wade was far from being my friend—I didn't even like him all that much—but I always felt bad for a bastard in trouble, because no matter whose face they wore, it always seemed to be me underneath.

"Y-yeah, Kev. I'm okay. Why?" His teeth chattered together briefly, from what I supposed was the chill of the rain, and he looked forward again. Something wasn't right. Wade wasn't acting sullen and depressed, which, for him, was normal.

"You sure?" I wanted to be compassionate—I thought of myself as a nice guy, who doesn't—but right then, more than anything I just wanted him out of my car. If he was on drugs, that was bad news. If it was something else, some deeper problem, I didn't want to know. I could think of myself as the nice guy all I wanted, but when it came down to it, I wanted to get Wade home, get back to my little room at Maverick House, and sleep the night away. Maybe that's selfish; probably that's selfish. But donuts, day in and day out, have a way of fatiguing you, believe it or not. I just didn't want trouble.

"Yeah. Listen, man, you don't mind giving me a ride, do you?" Wade looked at me with those jerky, spasmodic eyes again, and I began to feel a little worried. "Cause if you do, I can, like, walk. It's no big deal." But I saw in his eyes it was a big deal. His home was two miles away. He walked it in the good weather—why that didn't have any effect on his weight was lost on me—but in shit weather like this, there was no way. Even if I hated Wade, which I didn't, I wouldn't have made him walk home in this. I'm not *that* selfish. As if to emphasize my point, a roll of thunder boomed in the distance as we drove out of the Bear's parking lot.

"Can I turn on the radio?" he asked, and when he reached for the dial, I saw that his hand shook. He didn't wait for me to say yes before he flipped on the POWER button. The guitar buzz of Bruce Springsteen's "Adam Raised a Cain" filled the air of the car. That year, I'd discovered Bruce, and found out he was more than the poster boy of the mid-eighties. He was one of those singers that seemed to actually understand the unfortunate predicaments of me: the monotony of working at The Bear, the desperation of not going to college and not being able to find a girl, how driving your beat-up Chevy Impala was maybe the only thing that made you happy because, even though it was silly, it felt like escape. The tape I had in now was *Darkness on the Edge of Town*, which was a pretty apt description of where I was headed to that night, after I dropped Wade off and I was alone again.

Suddenly, Wade said, "You like The Bear, Kevin?" I was startled out of my reverie and asked him to repeat himself. Every time I drove him home, Wade had always been almost scarily silent. I'd tried to talk with him a few times—about girls, or about work, or anything. But he never spoke except for a scattered "yeah" or "naw" here or there. I kept trying, asking myself sometimes why I bothered.

"Not especially, why?" I asked him back. I turned down the radio a bit—the melancholy melody of "Factory" quieted—and glanced over at him. I could hear the steady whup-whup of the wipers on wet glass. It was a lonely sound.

He didn't answer, just asked, "What about your life? You like living in Maverick House?" By now, I was shocked. Not only was Wade talking in complete sentences, but it looked like—

"Wade, are you crying?" he looked away from me, embarrassed, his hand going up to his eyes. He shook his head violently back and forth. Rain splattered all over my face, and I reached up to wipe it off.

Uncomfortably, I said, "It's okay, man." This whole trip was going to hell on me—not that it had been a joyride at the start. I spent most of the day trying to avoid my own emotional problems; I had neither the capacity nor the inclination to deal with anyone else's.

"No, it's not okay!" Wade said, his face still in one big, meaty hand. "It's not!" He lifted up his other hand, and that's when I first saw the gun in it. The world stopped. There was the sound of rain and Springsteen and my own heart pounding in my ears. The world boiled down to this: a crying teenager had a gun in the passenger seat of my car, and the gun was pointed right at me.

"What the hell...?" I began, and Wade looked up. Tears—or maybe rainwater—dribbled down his big cheeks and made spots on the cloth of my seat. His hair hung in his eyes and he absently wiped a swatch of it away with his free hand. "It's not okay," he repeated, his breath now hitching in and out, as if in anticipation of a gigantic cry. I sat nearly paralyzed with fear, those twitchy eyes unnerving me almost as much as the gun. I was almost sure I had pissed my pants, but I couldn't really tell because rain and sweat had already drenched me from head to toe. For some time, I'd been wondering if I was even capable of grand emotions anymore, the rote monotony of my life at the Bear dulling me to the point of bland non-resistance. Wade at least answered that question: that dullness had been replaced with a terror so great I felt like I might choke on it.

"Nothing's okay, Kevin! Nothing! You don't walk up and down the streets at midnight, do you? You don't spend half your life sleeping outside, under the Blue River Bridge like some homeless guy, do you? *Do you*?"

"No, I..."

"I do, Kev. I come home and my mom tells me I'm a worthless piece of shit every night. Why don't you get a real job and support us, you worthless piece of shit, she asks me when I get in the door. She doesn't say it to my dad..." he hitched in another breath, and then the crying really did begin. "Because he's passed out when I get home at night. He's a *drunk*, Kev, can't you understand that?"

"For Christ's sake, put down the gun!" My eyes widened. His hand was trembling so badly I was afraid he'd pull the trigger without even meaning to.

Wade looked at the gun as if he were seeing it for the first time. Then, in a lightning flash movement I wouldn't have thought him capable of, he brought it up and touched the muzzle to his temple.

"You don't think I go to sleep at night, dreaming of girls I can't ever have? I know what I am, Kevin. I know my mom is right. I'm a fat, worthless piece of shit. I wake up, go work at Happy Fucking Bear, go home, listen to the piece of shit speech, pick my dad up off the floor and then go sleep under the Blue River Bridge. I usually have a few donuts left over from work I threw in my backpack, so I eat those. That's *dinner*."

My eyes darted from Wade to the road, and back to Wade again. I was looking for a way, some way to end this without one of us getting killed. And yet I heard him. Over the sound of the staccato drumbeat of rain on glass, and the plaintive cries of Springsteen singing about other, desperate people at other, desperate times, some of what Wade was saying got through.

I saw a turn in to a Burger King up ahead in the driving rain. It was familiar enough to me, even though the lights were all off inside. When I was younger, my mom and I used to drive out here and grab lunch; out back, the lawn sloped down toward Harwich Lake, and we used to sit on the grass and look at the lake and things were better once. These memories flashed by in under a second. It wasn't the lawn or the lake I was interested in now. I wanted the parking lot.

"And the thing is, Kev," he said quietly, his sobs dying a little, his shaking hand still gripping the gun tight against his head, "I can't see a way out. I can't. No way out of this shit I'm in."

The turn came. I took it, veering hard to the right and making Wade temporarily lurch backward. When he did, he lost grip of the gun. It fell into the back seat, landing on the empty Stop & Shop root beer cans scattered there.

I stopped the car and turned it off and ran out into the pouring rain. I reached Wade's side and yanked the door open. He was scrambling to reach the gun in the back, but his gut wasn't allowing him to reach far enough over the seat. I jerked him out of the car with all my strength, into the rain and onto the pavement of the Burger King parking lot.

That's when... look, I'm not proud of what I did. I'm not even sure why I did it. Anger was rushing in to replace my fear, but for those moments, the two existed in shaky balance. I fell to my knees and started slapping him as hard as I could, his cheeks making thick, meaty sounds as my palms connected. He was crying and I couldn't watch that, couldn't keep slapping his face while he sobbed like that. So I stood up, surveyed him a moment, and then started kicking him in the ass.

"You *bitch!*" I screamed at him, the rain obscuring my words. "You fucking *bitch!* A gun! A goddamn *gun!*" I kept repeating it over and over, calling him a bitch, kicking him in the ass. I don't know why. It was anger, and residual fear... but of course it was more than that. It was everything. My mother. Maverick House. The never-ending taste of Ramen noodles and cheap generic soda. My whole miserable life honed to this point, and for a bare moment I wondered why I'd been so desperate to preserve it when Wade had brought out the gun. I stood in the rain and I bitch-kicked this fucking guy. These aren't excuses. It's just what happened.

I stopped after a while and just looked at him lying there in the rain. He was crying and shaking, holding his legs up to his chest. I couldn't bear to watch that. It was just too wretched. I cried a little myself as I reached back into the car and retrieved the gun from the back seat.

When I brought it back out, Wade was looking at me with teary, hopeless eyes. I saw him minutely nod his head—*do it*, the nod said, *but please do it quickly. I deserve some mercy.* I looked at the gun for a second longer, then dashed across the lot to the lawn out back, the lawn on which my mother and I used to eat lunch before things got bad. I hurled the gun as far as I could into Harwich Lake, and even over the thunder noise of rain on the surface, I heard the gun splash down, now useless. No one here was going to die tonight.

I walked back to my car, sodden and exhausted. Wade still lay there on the pavement. When I offered my hand, I was sure he wouldn't take it, but after a moment, he did. I got him back in my car and brought him to Maverick House. We didn't talk. I gave him a towel and had him shower, and then put him in the baggiest clothes I had. That night he slept on my floor, and though it was technically against the rules, that's where he stayed for the next week and a half. When my landlord found out, he raised a few shades of holy hell, but I guess having someone sleep on my floor sort of paled in comparison to being a cannibal murderer, and all that happened was he kicked Wade out. That didn't last long. A few weeks later, I moved out, and Wade moved into the Murder Room.

The night of the gun was my last night at the Bear. The next morning I went in and quit, and I can't begin to tell you how freeing it is to cleanly cut the cord on something holding you back. I had some savings—not much—but it was enough to live on while I worked my ass off finding a better job. Some nights, coming home from hours stacked on hours, my desperation for work leaving me feeling empty and angry, I would lie on the floor and wish Wade was still here. We didn't say much to each other when he was here, but some nights I would turn on the stereo and we would listen to Springsteen and just take it easy for a little while. Taking it easy doesn't sound like a big deal, but we were both so unused to it that we drank it in greedily. Panic never seemed further from my mind as when Wade was there and the music was on.

Some night after he left, though, I got to wondering if maybe Wade hadn't had the best idea that night. I had fantasies about diving into the Harwich and finding that gun, trying to get it to work, trying to blow my brains out. Crazy thoughts, dark thoughts. I've never been great at what-next. Saving Wade had been my victory, and quitting the Bear was my *coup de grâce.* What next?

One morning I woke up with the residue of a dream clinging to me. It was Winston O'Brien, holding a big glass jug of milk in one hand, his eyes wide and crazy. In his other hand, he held the gun I had tossed away. It was trained on Wade, still soaking wet, sobbing on his knees in front of O'Brien. To my horror, I saw that Wade had no eyeballs; where they should have been were just endless black sockets, from which endless water poured. In the dream, O'Brien turns his gaze on me and says, very clearly, *"I'm so fucking hungry."* And then the gun goes off and I wake up, sweating and crying and panicked all over again.

There's a discount department store on the other side of town. After that horrible dream, I made my way there, working on impulse rather than coherent thought. They have a suit section, and I tried on a couple of used suits and bought them for twenty dollars each. The fact that they were still more than I could afford threatened to depress me, but I worked hard to keep that feeling at bay. That afternoon, I typed up a résumé using the library's computers (five cents per printed sheet—again, more than I could afford), using guide-books to map out my meager employment and educational history. When I was satisfied with it, I dressed in one of the thrift store suits and went to apply at EastWest Bank, the large branch down on Raven Street. Two weeks later, I became a teller.

It happened so fast, I could barely credit it. When you live in stagnation for so long, you start to feel like it's your only option. If you get stuck, you stay stuck. That's the way of the world, right? Only it's not. It took Wade's gun to remind me that I wanted to live. My only real roadblock was that I never really learned *how*. All that time at the Bear, I might have been waiting for someone to show me the best way to go about the business of living. The truth of it is, everyone else is trying to figure that out, too. They don't have time to show you how to climb out of the muck when they're all trying to do it themselves.

I moved out of Maverick House as soon as I could afford first and last somewhere better. I guess I wasn't really surprised when I found out Wade moved into my old room. In a way, I'm happy for him—he's going through the steps, just like I did. But God, I hope that he doesn't stay as long as I did. It's not just the fact of the murder that remains hanging over that room. A place like Maverick House thrives on despair, and despair smells like Ramen noodles and store-brand soda.

I went into the Happy Bear a couple days ago to get some coffee on my way to work. Wade isn't there anymore, either—I don't know where he works now. We've kind of lost touch. But that old, rusty, laughing bear still sits on the roof, grinning away and never moving. I bet he'll be there forever.

Not me. Not anymore. This kid's got places to go.

La Fenêtre du Grenier

"No," Doctor Peter Frakes said quietly, setting down his beer and looking at Edward with a smirk, "I don't believe in evil."

"Well, what about Jonestown? Or that weird sneaker guy?" Edward grabbed a handful of beer nuts and dropped them one by one into his mouth. *One thing I won't miss*, Peter thought, *is Edward's eating habits*.

"Both Heaven's Gate and Jonestown were cults, run by delusional men and fueled by even more delusional people. No evil there, just a case of mass psychosis."

"And serial killers? Jack the Ripper? Elmer Moody? How about Manson?"

"Just goes further in proving my point. Psychology. A dark variety of psychology, but that's it."

Edward was silent for a moment, and Peter looked around Dicey's Tavern for the last time. Ah, Dicey's. Always here when he needed to be alone, needed a second home. Needed a dark place to hide after Ellie died. He didn't much remember those dark, depressed months—months spent mostly at the bottom of a mug of Bud. But now the time had come to make up for all that, to both himself and Sadie. Stornetta, Nebraska. It had a nice ring.

"Okay, how about that house in England?" Edward asked, interrupting his reverie, "That 50 Berkley Street? The legend goes that sailors used to try to spend the night there when they couldn't get a hotel. They'd find them the next morning, rigid, a look of permanent fear on their face. Now, wouldn't you consider *that* evil?"

"Where do you get these stories, Ed?" Peter smiled indulgently, and took some beer nuts for himself. Edward could be childish, excitable, but Peter knew he'd miss his friend. During that dark time Edward had been at the house every day, to sober Peter up, to make sure Sadie never saw her daddy drunk. *I'm gonna miss you, buddy*, he thought sadly.

"Peter, this is fact. Listen, man, that house you're going to move into. I did some checking. Built in 1803 by "The Mad Frenchman," some guy named Marcel LaFayette. Some weirdo style called *fenêtre-non*."

"Yeah, the realtor told me. It means "no window." Except mine has one, in the attic."

"Well, did your realtor also tell you the house was a bordello in the late 1800s, until some crazy john slaughtered all the ladies of the evening one lurid night in June?"

"Lurid night in June, huh?"

"Okay, maybe August. Or that it was a speakeasy during Prohibition, until, of course, two guys got into a fight over some girl, and both of them, plus several onlookers wound up dead? Or that, as recently as 1987, an elderly couple participated in a murder-suicide pact *right in the living room*?"

"Ed, I know all this. You think I didn't do any research about my new house before I bought it, did you?"

"Well, no, I…"

"Every house has history, Ed. Not all of it is good. None of it has anything to do with the present."

"But Pete, the evidence is here. The recurrent nature of evil—it's cyclical. Evil comes in through the door, and sometimes you don't even know it until it's too late. Don't you even, for a moment, believe that a place, a house, can call evil into itself?"

Peter looked up from his mug, thought briefly of his sweet, lovely, dead wife, and said, "I already told you, Ed. I don't believe in evil."

* * *

"Is that it, Daddy?" Sadie asked, sticking her head out the window, her dark hair streaming back from her face in ribbons. Peter smiled at her. The car drifted by a sign on the right reading WELCOME TO STOR-NETTA, NEBRASKA. *No population marker, I see,* Peter thought.

"That's it, honey. Our new home."

The house stood solitarily on the long, barren street. It rose up like a giant, silent beast, a blue and white monolith among the cornfield flatlands. The lawn surrounding it was trim, neat, a quiet row of flowers edging the base of the house. Roses and tulips blossomed brightly from a dual flower garden on either side of the front walk, a flagstone path leading to the large, stately front door. The front face of the house stood blank, unyielding, broken only by the door at the bottom. As they drove closer, Peter looked to the right side of house, and there, up near the top, was the single window. The attic window.

"Daddy, it looks like a barn," Sadie said, but she was smiling. Peter laughed.

"Yeah, I guess it does, doesn't it. It's blue, though, not red."

"Why aren't there any windows? That's really weird."

"There is one, Sade," he said, and pointed.

"Oh."

Peter parked the car at the curb and got out, stretching. Sadie flung her door open and ran merrily up the flagstone path, playing intermittent hopscotch with the irregularly shaped stones. A grin came over Peter's face, and he thought, *This is home. Really home.*

"Daddy! The door's locked!"

"Okay, hold your horses." He jogged up the path, tempted to play hopscotch himself, then thought better of it. That stuff was for kids, and he certainly wasn't a kid anymore. But did that matter? He wasn't impressing anyone here, he wasn't in a stuffy doctor's lounge full of exhausted, grim surgeons who weren't in the mood for fun. Finally, he was alone with his daughter, the only person that really mattered to him anymore. He wouldn't be enrolling her in first grade for another whole month, and his new career at Edwinton Medical the next town over didn't begin for a week after that. Until then... freedom. Stornetta, this house, it was more than a place to start over. It was freedom.

"Hey, Sadie, watch this," he said, and did a fumbling, awkward cartwheel, falling on his butt in the left-side flower garden. Sadie shrieked with laughter.

"Ow," he said, picking himself up gently and pulling the stalk of a rose gingerly from his shirt sleeve. Sadie only laughed harder. Peter smiled back. This was going to be good.

That was when the front door opened, swinging inward seemingly by itself, and Sadie screamed.

* * *

Peter supposed, that night in bed, that it was the type of thing he would laugh about later. Probably he and Sadie both, when the years got behind and he started to think of her as an adult instead of just his daughter. But not today, not when it counted, when there was an impressionable girl of seven scared half to death, and a man of almost forty just as frightened.

The way the door opened, that inward swing—it brought back to mind the conversation he'd had with Ed just before he and Sadie took off. *Evil comes in through the door*, he'd said, *and sometimes you don't even know it until it's too late.* But what if it was already here, waiting to spring? What if Ed's wildly creative mind was more correct about this house than his own logical one? And what, exactly, was opening the door?

Sadie had screamed; he had screamed. Then, a startled, confused-looking old man had stepped out, his hands raised in an *I-ain't-armed* gesture. "Doctor Frakes?" the old party had asked, his voice sounding rough and a bit weary. "Doctor Peter Frakes?"

Peter had caught his breath, finally. The light asthma that had afflicted him since he was Sadie's age had come on strong for a moment, but the spell had passed. "Yes, that's me," he said, his mind reeling. Who the hell was this? "May I ask what you're doing in my house?"

"I'm Bernard Knowles," the old man said, taking a hesitant step toward Peter, lowering his hands and sticking one out. "I assumed Ms. Clark had spoken to you about me?"

Suddenly, light dawned in Peter's mind: of course! Mr. Knowles! The *housekeeper!*

"Oh, I am so sorry, Mr. Knowles," Peter had said, feeling a rosy blush creep up from his collar. "Yes, the realtor told me about you, I... God, I feel foolish."

"No need to, friend," Knowles had said, grasping Peter's right hand in his own. The man's skin felt weathered and dry—somehow very *old*, much older than the man's fiftyish appearance—and Peter resisted an urge to pull his hand away fast. The sensation was unpleasant. "If I had seen that door swing open like that, I would have screamed like all get out."

Now, Peter smiled in the dark, trying to sleep for the first time in his new, absurdly spacious house. Trying to forget Sadie's terrified face, the same face she had made when she had found her mother lying on the floor of the bathroom in their apartment in Queens, Ellie's wrists hacked to shreds, the mirror above the sink broken into pieces, Ellie screaming and Sadie shrieking, blood everywhere. Trying to forget all about that past life, that old life, those old thoughts.

They were in Stornetta now, in an actual *house*, and the dark days were past.

But unconsciously, his mind reproached that thought, for with no windows in this room, or any room, dark pervaded like a living thing. It was dark that floated around him as he dove into the deep chamber of sleep, only to be greeted by the blackness of a night without dreams.

* * *

Two weeks passed, weeks crammed with the cacophony of moving in. Knowles proved to be very helpful, lugging in furniture from the moving trucks right along with the movers, organizing the boxes by room (each box had been written on in Peter's careful, cramped print: P. BEDROOM, S. BEDROOM, BATH, KITCHEN, et cetera.) The day after Peter and Sadie moved in, he disappeared for a couple of hours, only to return in his battered, ancient Jeep with eight bags of groceries. It was odd, almost prescient, how Knowles knew which foods to get, from Peter's Romaine lettuce and wheat germ to Sadie's favorite cereals, Boo Berry and Count Chocula.

"This is all on the tab?" Peter asked, coming into the large oak-centric kitchen and helping the old man put away the food.

"I'm used to a weekly budget for the house's supplies," Knowles said, placing three cans of tomato soup—Sadie's favorite—into a high cupboard. "This should last us about two weeks, maybe three. Between then and now, we can draw up a plan for you and the little girl." Knowles stopped, looking at Peter with wide eyes. "I didn't do wrong by this, did I? I just assumed..."

"No, no, Mr. Knowles, not at all. You did fine here. I guess I'm just not used to people doing my shopping for me."

"Not only is it my job, Mr. Frakes, it's my pleasure. I suppose I should inform you of the other weekly and monthly expenses, as well."

"Later," Peter said, opening up the refrigerator and placing two gallon jugs of orange juice on the top shelf. "Paperwork can wait. I'm sure we'll work together well; you already seem to know our favorite foods."

Knowles gave him an odd look. Peter thought it was slightly defensive. "Not at all, Mr. Frakes. I just... have an understanding of people, is all. I guess certain things."

"Second sight?" Peter asked, grinning a little but not joking. He did believe in higher levels of thought—clairvoyance, precognition, extrasensory perception. His belief had nothing to do with a deep knowledge of the occult, or even of faith, but such things had been proven too many times by too many scientific methods to be complete hokum. But he had never actually met someone....

"No," Knowles said, a little sharply. "I just know things, that's all, Mr. Frakes."

Peter nodded slightly, not willing to press the man any further on what seemed to be a difficult subject. "By the way, please call me Peter," he said, smiling, and sticking out his hand.

"Peter it is, then," Knowles returned, grasping the man's hand. Peter noticed the man made no offer of his own first name.

"Yes, well," Peter said, breaking the handshake and heading for the door. "I guess I'll go help Sadie unpack her things." He pressed his hand to the door, when Knowles stopped him.

"Mr. Frakes!" he stage-whispered. Peter spun around, and that was when all conscious thought left him. Knowles stood before him, his hand on a box of Fruity Pebbles, but it was not Knowles anymore. His other hand, now ancient, bony, arthritic, gripped a gnarled wooden cane, the head of which was topped with a frightening ouroboros figure: a bloated snake eating its own tail. The man's body was now draped in sack-like robes, extending down over his legs and lying in a brown puddle on the floor of the kitchen, his head now hidden by a dark, obscuring hood. Around his neck hung a metallic medallion, and Peter saw with perfect clarity that it was the symbol of the snakes twisted around a cane: the symbol of a doctor.

"Mr. Frakes, you must go!" the man said, his voice haggard and weary.

"Who are you?" Peter asked, his voice cracking, his eyes wide with terror.

"I am the Cleric of the Doorway. I must warn you, I must try to stop it!"

"Stop what? What doorway?"

"You are in the web, doctor. You are not here! Do you understand me? You are in the web, and the web *is not here!*"

Peter stood transfixed, unable to move, to speak. His head spun in delirious circles.

"The doorway inside is a passageway through," the Cleric said, not raising his head. "But the *window—* Mr. Frakes, the *window is the real gateway.*" The main looked up, touched his hand to his hood, and began to remove it. Peter saw one glimpse of flesh, bald, putrescent, maddening, and then he heard Sadie's cries from the next room, calling for her daddy.

Peter looked to the door, then back at Knowles. The old man was putting away a clear plastic container of sprouts.

"Did you hear something?" Peter asked the man, desperately trying to remember something, but ultimately losing it.

"Your little girl seems to be calling for you, Peter," Knowles said, looking up. Peter thought he could read the same look of something just-forgotten on the man's face, when Sadie called again. He pressed on the door, letting it swing out, and went to find his daughter.

* * *

Sadie stood on the small loveseat in the living room, her eyes wide, a finger extended to a far-off corner across the room. For a brief moment, Peter's past intermingled with the present: Sadie had been conceived on that loveseat, during a particularly sweaty night of lovemaking. A surge of grief coursed through Peter, and that old familiar shame of not knowing anything was wrong with his wife in the weeks or months before her suicide. Then he shook himself out of it and turned his attention to his daughter, who was still alive and, at present, screaming her lungs out.

"What is it, Sade?" he asked, a furrow of concern wrinkling his brow.

"A buggy! A gross one with a lot of legs!"

Peter shivered minutely. Sadie may have gotten her blue eyes and black hair from Ellie, but apparently she received his dread of many-legged buggies. Cautiously, he approached the corner, grabbing some loose newspaper from a box by the loveseat.

"Do you see it, Daddy?" the girl asked, her voice much steadier now that Daddy had everything under control. He couldn't wait until she had kids, so that when one of them got scared of a gross buggy....

Then he saw it—a centipede squirming around in the corner, seemingly trying to burrow. His eyes locked onto it, and he gripped the paper tighter in his hand. Then—*then*—it seemed to *change*.

Not a centipede, but *what*? Its legs moved at odd, restless angles, all in different directions. Its body

—not solid, not liquid, not gaseous—

what the *hell*? Its body seemed to writhe, to mutate, changing form every nanosecond. Peter looked, stared, and somehow knew that the centipede

—not a centipede, Peter, you know that—

or whatever it was *in* its true form—not solid, not liquid, not gaseous. Something else, something just out of the reach of his mind. Something...

Then his eyes began to burn, and his head throbbed dully. His hands went to his face, blocking the image of the bug out. After a few moments, the throbbing resided, and he let his hands drop. The bug was gone.

Sadie was tugging at his jeans, looking up at him with wide, inquisitive eyes.

"Are you okay, Daddy?" she asked, and he saw that same furrow of concern on her brow. Like Dad, like daughter, he thought.

"Yeah, Sade-er-oo," he said, tousling her hair. For once, she didn't duck away. Instead, she pointed to the corner again.

"Dad, was that thing real?"

He thought later it might have been her somber tone. The question seemed to hold the weight of the world even in the mouth of his six-year-old-daughter. Or maybe it had been the fact that she called him Dad instead of Daddy, a first. In any case, he made the decision to tell her the complete truth without even consulting his own mind first.

"I don't know, honey," he said, looking into the corner himself. "I really don't know."

* * *

Several days after what Peter termed in his mind "The Buggy Incident," the house was finally livable. The furniture which had looked so huge in Queens now was dwarfed by the high, peaked ceilings and the forever-extending walls. Sadie's toys were scattered all over the place as usual, but now they seemed less underfoot. What was more, Peter was beginning to see less and less of Sadie—there were dozens of rooms in this house, all waiting for eager six-year old eyes to explore them. The fact that some of those rooms had been once used as places of commerce for ladies of the evening and their johns only bothered him a little. Sadie didn't know that, and probably never would.

Peter's job didn't officially begin for another month or so, and he had planned to spend the time reading. That experiment hadn't worked out as well as he had expected. The quiet got to him—the downshift from the cacophony of Queens to the almost deathly silence of this tiny little Nebraska town was a bit disconcerting. He tried the reading some of the classics that had somehow eluded during his high school and college years: *Heart of Darkness, A Tale of Two Cities, 1984.* But Conrad seemed to have trouble connecting scenes, Dickens was a tad too dry for his taste, Orwell too paranoid. Trying to delve into the modern works proved to little avail as well. Robert Parker's Spenser seemed wildly out of place given Peter's surroundings, Crichton was too much medical jargon than he wanted right now, and a brief glimpse through King's *The Shining* made him come to the conclusion that the hotel in that book was just too close to his new house for comfort.

What really sparked him were his bedtime readings to his daughter. He had relived the magical worlds of Alice through Sadie, who enjoyed them every bit as much as he did as a child. Currently, they were traveling through the Chronicles of Narnia—the first book in the series excited Sadie to no end.

"I want to be like Lucy!" she exclaimed when the little girl in the book first opened the passageway to the cold, magical world of Narnia. "I'm going to explore the entire house until I find another world!" Peter had smiled indulgently, but her words had set something off in his mind as well. He had nothing better to do: why not tour the whole house by himself? Who knew what he might find?

The thought had led him to this door, four days later. It was tucked away in a corner on the west side of the house, at the end of a long, narrow hallway. Peter smiled a bit wanly, placing his hand on the doorknob. Ellie had loved places like this—before Sadie was born, the two of them liked to go to amusement parks. Without fail, Ellie would drag him into the Maze of Mirrors first thing, before the roller coasters and the funhouse and the Tilt-a-Whirl. She had loved the Maze of Mirrors, giggling when she got lost and bumped into a wall, stopping to make faces in the warped and bubbled mirrors set into the passageway out. Peter had indulged her, but the mirrors always made him queasy. He didn't like the idea of getting stuck where you couldn't get out, and he hated getting lost. He remembered once when he seemed closed in on all sides, glancing around in a glassy kind of panic, seeing his sweaty, wild-eyed face everywhere he turned. He had tried calling for Ellie, but she was laughing her way out of the Maze far, far away.

He had eventually gotten himself out, but he never forgot that stab of horror, the sudden, exquisitely terrible knowledge that he would be stuck here forever and ever, staring at himself in desperate multiple until he went mad.

Then why am I here and Ellie not? He thought, the brass doorknob growing warm under his hand. *Why am I in the Maze now, only in a Maze of Doors, and Ellie ended up smashing the mirror and slitting her wrists with the pieces? Does that make any sense?*

He inhaled deeply—a long, shuddery gasp. It didn't make any sense at all, but there it was. Such was life. Babies are born, old men die, and sometimes wives commit suicide. *C'est la vie.*

Peter opened the door.

It opened wide on a large, dark room. Without windows, all the rooms were dark—but this one seemed a little blacker than the rest. He reached an experimental hand to the right of the doorway, feeling around until his fingers touched a toggle switch. He flipped it, and suddenly light illuminated the place. The room, not as gigantic as the living room but still huge, was paneled in a rich mahogany, deepening the darkness the room still seemed to be made of. A massive claw-footed oak table dominated the center of the room, and two large, overstuffed easy chairs stood sentry at the far end corners. There was a seemingly half-finished game of white varnished dominoes played out by the edge of the table. But Peter noticed none of that, not at first.

The room was filled from floor to ceiling with books. The shelves, set into the walls, towered over him. Peter doubted if there were this many books in the Edwinton library, where he had picked up the Narnia books for Sadie and his own failed selections. One foot stepped over the raised wooden bumper and a sudden thought—

the realtor hadn't mentioned any library, Peter, had she?

—came and passed and he was in the library. His eyes wide, Peter surveyed the selections. A King James Bible that looked old enough to have been owned by King James himself, what seemed a complete leather-bound set of the works of Shakespeare (he found similar collections of Twain and DuMaurier further down the first wall) and a remarkably pristine copy of *Beowulf,* at the rightmost edge of the lower shelf. He plucked it out, marveling briefly at the still sharp wood-cut design on the front cover and leafed to the copyright page. The Roman numerals at the bottom of the page gave the copyright year as 1769.

"Oh wow," Peter said, too stunned to utter anything else.

Slowly, he walked along the length of the left wall, trailing one light finger over the ancient volumes, marveling at the seemingly timeless quality of these books. It was as if they had been sealed in an airtight compartment, kept exactly as they had been when they were published. It seemed impossible, but here it was, take it or leave it.

Peter caught a bright spot of red in his peripheral vision, and he followed his gaze. Top shelf, far book-case: a slim, unprofessional book bound in red leath-er. Curious, Peter went to it; it was so high up he had to stand on one of the chairs tucked under the giant table to reach it. He pulled it down, sat on the chair in front of the game of dominoes, and opened the book.

He read for six hours.

* * *

From the Dyarie of Marcel LaFayette, entry dated 12/04. Year unknown.

...they called to me again last night. The shifting people. I can hear them, every now and again, scutter-ing against the outer walls. In their mad ramblings, I hear my name being called, as if I am being summoned. To what place, what ungodly realm these people dwell in. I am not insane, I tell myself, night after night. Sure-ly, I cannot be insane. I am an architect. Architects do not go insane—that is the work of writers, artists, and actors.

But oh! Dear God, their moans are maddening! As I close my eyes at night, I hear them, thumping against the wall of my bedroom, and the thumps sound so large, they sound so hideously large! And I have dreams. Dreams of an old man who refers to himself as "The Cleric." He seems benevolent, but the dreams disperse before I can get any clear picture.

I thank God that I built the house with no windows. I do not want to see. I do not want to know what is out there. Sometimes I wish I could leave this god-awful place. Yet, something holds me, something binds me here. My work, built on soil I own. I cannot leave this creation. I cannot leave this house....

* * *

When Peter looked up, his eyes burning from the read, his head hurting, he glanced over at the game of dominoes. Had they perhaps moved since he opened the book? They looked different, somehow.

Shaking his head, realizing that sounded silly (but perfectly reasonable against the lunacy of LaFayette's words), he left the diary on the table and walked, a little shaken, out of the room.

* * *

Christmas Eve, and Van Morrison was on the CD player, turned up as loud as possible. Knowles sat in the corner, watching the doctor and his daughter dancing around in circles. Peter waved a come-on gesture to Knowles, urging him to join. Knowles shook his head and sipped more hot cider. The old man looked exhausted.

Not that Peter was thinking about his housekeeper much. His mind was on Sadie, and Christmas, and getting the best out of this time. It was the first Christmas without his wife, and Peter was still unsure how he felt about that.

But that didn't mean he had to dwell on it, not now.

"We used to sing!" he shouted to Sadie. She joined in the sha-la-la chorus, breaking into giggles halfway through. Peter picked her up and tossed her gently into the air (still marveling that it was possible to do that, still feeling demure in this giant place). Sadie shrieked with laughter, and Peter joined her. This was it: this was the time of joy he'd been waiting for. Thoughts of his wife and Queens and being a doctor— none of that mattered now. All that mattered was the joy in Sadie's face. Her—

face suddenly shifted, twisted, into a dark, malev-
olent maw, an insect's face that chirped and burred,
but even then not an insect's face, shifting, turning,
squelching together and driving him mad, it's a buggy,
all right, but not a normal buggy, not a normal daugh-
ter, has she seen the Outside I wonder, does she know
the secrets, has she been to la fenêtre du grenier kind
sir read on read on

—eyes looking concerned as he dropped her suddenly, falling to the floor.

"Doctor Frakes!" Knowles called out, running to
him. "Doctor Frakes are you all right?"

Sadie sat down across from him, crying a little.
The crying was more in shock than pain, he knew,
but hurt gripped his heart just the same. Ellie had
done a lot of crying in the later days. He could never
understand why.

Just as now, he couldn't understand what had
happened.

"Sade? You okay?" She answered quietly. Peter
didn't hear. Quickly, he got up off the floor and snapped
off Van Morrison, right in the middle of "Domino."

"What, honey?"

"I said why'd you drop me?"

"I didn't mean to, sweetie. I think I

– blacked out—

tripped or something. Are you hurt?"

She shook her head. From behind their crouched
place on the floor, a loud, relieved sigh issued. Peter
turned. It was Knowles.

What an odd little family we make, Peter thought
suddenly.

"Good that you're all right, little miss," Knowles
said, his hands on his knees.

Now she smiled a little, and everything was all
right again.

Peter looked at the clock hanging above the door leading into the kitchen. "Oh, boy, Sadie, I think it's time for little girls to get into bed."

Sadie stood up, frowning a little, but Peter could see the barely-concealed excitement of Christmas on her face.

"Daddy!" she protested.

Peter smiled. Growing up in New York, he had never had a real Christmas. One year, his father had come into his bedroom drunk, his Department of Sanitation uniform still on and reeking of waste and alcohol, and he'd handed Peter a beer. "Merry Christmas," he'd said, then passed out on Peter's floor. Peter had been eight.

Ever since he was a boy, he vowed to make Christmas a special day for his own family, if he ever got one. Now, his family number had been reduced... but in a way, it hadn't. They had Knowles, didn't they?

"Okay, you can open one present tonight, but then to bed."

Sadie shrieked with delight, running over to the gigantic tree and selecting a small box wrapped in cartoon-character paper. Holding it high, she came jogging back to him, the white cotton nightie trailing out behind her.

"Can I open this one, Daddy?"

"You sure can."

She plopped down in front of him, tearing into the paper, shredding it in her little hands. Underneath was a flat brown box. Sadie looked up at her father with wide, expectant eyes, and lifted the cover to the box. She gasped as she looked inside. Peter smiled. By God, he'd gotten it right.

"Oh, Daddy, thank you!"

"Do you want to try it on?" She nodded.

He lifted the barrette out gently and set the box aside. It was brown and mottled, like the tortoise-shell comb in that book *The Gift of the Magi*.

Also like the one Sadie's mother wore when she was buried.

Sadie had loved her mother's hair barrettes, and Ellie would let her play with them if she'd been good. Ellie had told Peter once that the barrettes were her only sin of vanity. She had collected them as teenage boys collect baseball cards, had had jewelry boxes full of them back at their apartment in Queens. She was wearing her favorite barrette when she had sliced her wrists open in the bathroom, and it was the one she wore to her grave. It had also been Sadie's favorite, and the night after the funeral, Sadie had wept bitterly for both the loss of her mother and of her mother's best-loved thing.

Now, as Peter secured her long black hair with it, he thought of how stunningly she looked like Ellie, and how much he still missed his wife.

"Okay, now," he said, holding back a choked sob. "Off to bed, Sader-oo."

She ran off up the stairs. Peter put his hands to his face and wept a little. After some time, he felt a hand on his shoulder, a comforting hand. Knowles.

He dropped his hand and turned to face the housekeeper, but it wasn't Knowles anymore.

The figure stood before him, and now Peter remembered, remembered in the kitchen. Knowles had appeared before him in cloaks, but it hadn't been Knowles then, had it? No. It had been The Cleric.

"Close your *eyes!*" the Cleric commanded. Peter obeyed. From somewhere distant, Peter could hear a vague rumbling. No, that wasn't right. Not *hear*, exactly, because you couldn't hear anything here. What...?

"This is part of where we are," the Cleric said in his age-worn, leathery voice. "Not where you perceive we are, not among the walls and ceilings you consider *home.*"

Peter tried to answer but felt suddenly lightheaded, and a curious weightless sensation took him over.

"We are sheathed in darkness," The Cleric told him, the cloak still shrouding his face. "Don't open your eyes. To see into the darkness is madness, Doctor. Run from the darkness, run into the light. Take the girl and run into a lighted world."

"I don't understand!" Peter said, but his voice felt empty and hollow to his own ears. Suddenly, a swatch of light appeared behind the man—the Cleric—and for a split second, Peter thought he understood *everything*.

Then the darkness collapsed and Peter and Knowles stood facing each other by the Christmas tree in the large house in Stornetta, Nebraska.

"Was there a blackout, Knowles?" Peter asked, his mind desperate to remember something. He saw the same look of abstract puzzlement on Knowles's face.

"I—I believe so, sir, for a moment or two. I'll check the fuses."

Peter shook his head. "No need. It's Christmas Eve. Go up to your room and sleep."

Knowles smiled and bowed his head a little. "Thank you, Doc—Peter. Good night."

Peter watched him walk up the stairs, plodding in his old-man's way. Peter smiled after him, but for a brief moment he wondered

—where do you sleep Knowles? Where do you sleep? In a room upstairs or is it in a dark pocket, an unlit world, something not... quite... here—

Then the migraine came, blasting his skull from the inside, battering his mind, driving him to his knees on the floor, dwarfed by the tree. Pressing his palms to his eyes, he wept in pain for nearly five minutes before he felt well enough to go upstairs to bed.

* * *

Three days before New Year's Eve. It would be the beginning of a brand new year in a new house with a new life. Sadie would be going to school, Peter would be going to work, and life would resume as peacefully as it had been before Ellie had died.

Now, though, now was time for the library.

The day after Christmas, Peter had woken at five in the morning to sounds of rustling. *Birds*, he thought, *or a squirrel, trapped in the walls.* He'd had no idea how to deal with such a problem, and vowed to himself to ask Knowles about it at a more civil hour. At that, he'd had every intention of going back to sleep. Then, he thought he heard Ellie's voice, his dead wife's voice, calling him.

"Ellie?" he'd asked aloud, and threw back the bed sheets. All he wore were a pair of boxer shorts underneath, and the room was somehow cold, cold. The voice didn't respond.

"Ellie?" he repeated, wishing to look outside to see if he could be mistaking the "voice" for something else. Of course, he couldn't look outside. No windows.

Instead, he went to his door on the other side of the room and opened it. "Ellie?" he asked, his voice trembling. "Ellie, is that you?"

His mind whispered back, *This isn't a ghost story, Peter, and you damn well know it.*

No, not a ghost story. Not at all.

The voice stopped calling. For a moment, Peter stood on the door jamb, telling himself to go back to bed. Then came that curious scuttering sound from the walls behind him again, and he decided he didn't want to sleep in there anymore tonight.

The hallways were dark. At six AM, Knowles would turn on the lights and begin making breakfast, but six AM was a long time coming. Peter padded down the hallway in his bare feet, looking ahead blindly, not aware where he was going. He made a turn. Another. And suddenly he was at the door of the library.

Don't go in, Pete, a voice whispered in his mind. Again, it was the voice of Ellie, but this time it was different, softer, more like her usual voice than that of the spectral summoning that had woken him. This voice was the voice she had used in the tender moments, before the depressed periods when he was too busy working to see she needed help. This was his perfect memory-voice of hers, and for a moment his hand trembled near the doorknob.

But his mind itched to read more of LaFayette's diary, and that pull was too strong to resist. He put his hand on the doorknob, and stepped inside.

* * *

The light switches, installed nearly a hundred years after the house was built, were on the left side of the door, and Peter flicked all five on at once. The library lit up like day and Peter shielded his eyes. When he finally lowered his arm, he saw something on the large center table that hadn't been there before, replacing the game of dominoes next to the diary he had left on the table last time. He looked closer. It was a chess set.

"Knowles probably put it out," Peter said, not believing himself but lacking the capacity to believe otherwise. "Dominoes, chess. Games of skill." He went to the chess set, touching the black-and-red board with one slightly trembling finger. When had it gotten cold in here?

Choosing the seat he had sat in before, he tweezed one of the pieces—a white pawn—in his fingers and moved it two spaces. Dropping it, he rubbed his fingers on his boxer shorts. He hadn't liked the feel of the piece in his hand. It had felt... *slimy* somehow.

He picked up the diary he had left on the table before, and thumbed to the last entry he had read. Soon, he was again absorbed. The man who had built this house had steadily gone insane, and he had documented all of it. It was darkly fascinating.

When he looked up from the book, four hours later, his eyes (and head) hurt. He put the book down and stood, about to go to the door, but something caught his eye, something not quite right.

It took him a full minute, but then he saw. On the chess board, an opposing piece, a black pawn, had moved forward two spaces, mirroring his.

"No," he said quietly, shaking his head.

Yes, the voice in his head said, and this time it held no pretenses of being his dead wife's: this voice was dark and scuttery and *crawling* at the back of his mind.

"*No!*" he said, raising his hand and smashing the chess pieces with the back of his hand. He turned to walk—*run*, actually—out of the room, when searing pain shot through his hand and he screamed.

He raised his hand and stared in horror at it. One of the chess pieces, a black knight, had latched onto his index finger... and was *biting*.

Peter screamed, flailing his hand back and forth. His eyes stared wildly at it as it moved with his hand. It was the head of a horse, a knight... and then it wasn't. Everything seemed to slow down, go frame by frame like a movie in slow motion. He saw the knight as a regular chess piece, with long black horse-teeth clamping down on his finger. Then, *flash*: it was twisting, melting, it wasn't solid or liquid or gaseous, it was something *other*, and this was not a ghost story, no, Peter, this was *far worse*...

His eyes began to burn and Peter shrieked, clamping his other hand over his eyes. He couldn't look, for to look would be madness. Blindly, he felt around the surface of the large table for LaFayette's diary, finally gripping it by the front cover. He threw his pained hand—now bleeding, he could feel, the agony as sharp as needles—to the table surface and began beating it with the book.

Different pain seared through his hand, meaty, throbbing pain. An oboe of bruising bones and swelling muscles to accompany the piccolo of the puncture wound. Down again, another slap of the book on his index finger, and though he was sure it wasn't broken, it certainly felt sprained. The knight hung on, biting harder. Again, *slap*, again, *slap*, again, again, again, and finally the piece loosened its grip, releasing his finger. Peter took his other hand from his eyes just in time to see the scurrying piece flail around dizzily and topple off the table's edge. He only glimpsed its movements for a second, but even then it was almost too much. What had been a chess piece had become something completely incomprehensible. Peter tried to wrap his mind around it and succeeded only in getting a headache. His eyes hurt, burning again. What he had seen was not meant to be seen by human eyes. To look at it too long would be an exercise in madness.

Without looking anywhere but straight ahead, Peter bolted for the door in his bare feet, bulleting into the hallway and slamming the library door behind him.

The lights were on now, and dimly he was aware that he was very nearly naked. He stood against the wall opposite the door to the library and closed his eyes against this light.

What is going on here? There'd been dominoes there before, and I don't think Knowles changed the sets. Chess pieces that bite, bugs that change shape, dead wives who call in the middle of the night, what the hell is all this?

"The book," he muttered, and opened his eyes. That was *it*! LaFayette's diary of madness was getting to him, that was all. That...

He glanced down at his finger and saw a trickle of blood racing from the tip.

Rationalize that, Peter, he thought, and might have begun doing so when Knowles turned the corner at a cheetah's pace and ran wide-eyed up to Peter.

"Knowles, what is it?" Peter asked, his fingers throbbing, blood puddling to the carpet. The man was heaving breath in and out, unable to catch it. Peter looked into the man's pale face and grabbed him by the shoulders. His blood soaked into Knowles's white shirt, dyeing it pink.

"*What is it?*"

"It's the... girl, your daughter," Knowles managed.

"What about her?" Peter asked, his voice smaller now, his brain locking into overdrive.

"I can't find her, Doctor," Knowles said. "Sadie's missing."

* * *

Peter dashed back to his room to throw on a jogging suit, calling out his daughter's name the whole time. She didn't respond, but that wasn't totally disheartening. She could be anywhere in the house. It was a big house. A person could scream at the top of their lungs at one end of the house and no one could hear them at the other end. Peter's mind flashed on the chess piece that bit, and the ravings of Lafayette in the journal, and suddenly the idea of a person screaming to an unhearing audience terrified him.

"*Sadie!*" he cried, running down the hallway toward her room. He threw open the door and ran inside.

Her four-poster bed was messy, but made. Helford, her teddy bear, sat up on her pillow, staring at the world with blank polar-bear eyes. The floor was strewn with coloring books and Little Golden Books; Sadie could read most of those by herself. Colored Lego pieces were scattered around, the remnants of what may have been a Lego house near the large plastic toy box in the far corner.

"Sadie?" Peter asked. His daughter didn't answer him, but he again heard that *scratching* sound he'd heard in his bedroom early this morning. The scratching that sounded like a trapped animal wanting to get out.

He went to the bed and raised the ruff. A few dolls and more Golden Books under here, but no Sadie.

Scratch-scratch-scraaaaatch.

Unnerved, Peter went to the toy box, his heart sinking a little. Could someone suffocate in there? Taking in a breath, he grabbed the lid, and threw it open. She wasn't there, either.

"Sadie?"

Scratch.

Fear gripped him now. He wanted to leave this room, it felt dead, it felt hideously *used up*, but it was a fairly big room, and maybe she was hiding in her closet.

"Sadie, please honey, where are you?"

Scraaaaaaaatch, and Peter turned to face it because it sounded bigger this time. Meatier. He looked toward the wall, the far wall he'd just been near with the toy box. There was a crack in that wall. It hadn't been there before.

"Oh Jesus," Peter whispered.

Scratch.

Not the sound of a trapped animal trying to get out, no, oh God, but something out there *trying to get in.*

Peter screamed and bolted from the room, slamming Sadie's door behind him. He ran toward the stairs, trying to call out his daughter's name but his voice got lost in a high fear-pitch of incoherence.

Knowles was in the living room at the bottom of the stairs. The Christmas tree loomed up behind him, dwarfing him. Worry lines creased his brow.

"Sadie!" Peter yelled, getting some composure back, jogging past Knowles toward the kitchen.

"Peter, I've looked...," Knowles began but Peter didn't hear the rest. He was in the kitchen, staring at the little counter by the large stove. There was a stool pulled up to the side, and a half-eaten bowl of cereal on the counter. One of Sadie's bad habits, never finishing a meal, but that had been something she picked up from her mother. Peter's heart twisted again, and he walked over to the bowl on the counter.

Some multicolored sugar bits floated in the milk, Sadie's Disney spoon sticking out of the remains. A single tear dribbled from Peter's eye, and plopped down into the bowl.

Don't stop, you idiot, she's just missing, now go find *her*, an interior voice, perhaps Ellie's, screamed. Peter ignored it for the moment. What did Ellie know, anyway? She was dead.

Peter picked up the bowl with trembling fingers, put the curve to his lips, and drank. The milk tasted sickly-sweet, wonderful on his tongue.

"Peter." A voice from behind. Peter closed his eyes. "Peter." His eyes still closed, Peter turned. He knew this voice, this familiar voice. It was the voice of the Cleric.

"Do you understand now?" the voice asked. "This house is not part of your world. The door is the passageway. You came through easily. You may be able to leave just as easily. Before it's too late, before your forget, save yourself, Peter."

"What about my daughter?" Peter asked. There was no response. "*What about my daughter!*" he screamed, and Knowles answered.

"I still haven't found her, sir." Peter opened his eyes and Knowles stood there in the harsh kitchen light, looking as scared as Peter felt.

Something was slipping away from him now, something he desperately needed to remember. What...?

Save yourself.

"Knowles?" he asked, and he saw that a glazed, far away look had come into the housekeeper's eyes. He was muttering something.

Peter crossed the room and came close to him. "What are you saying?"

His eyes still glazed, almost hypnotic, Knowles whispered, "I am a passageway, too. For the other one. But he failed. We failed. We're not strong enough."

Peter's eyes went wide. He tried to say something but his mouth wouldn't work. Instead, he moved on rubbery legs toward the kitchen door and back out into the living room.

His daughter was at the top of the stairs. Her hair was snow white and the same glazed look was in her eyes. Peter screamed, running toward the stairs, running up to her. When he saw her, his scream died in his throat. It was too big to release.

Sadie's face was no longer her own. It was twisted, her little-girl mouth a red knot in her jaw. Her eyes were wide, swimming in their sockets; they looked as if they had been short-circuited with terror. A small trickle of blood ran down from her nose. She stood, mute, not seeing anything.

"Sadie," he said softly, tears streaming from his eyes, pulling her close to him. "Oh, my little girl."

Then, she began shrieking.

"Out... there! Ch-ch-ch! Out the WINDOW, it's the WINDOW! Ft-ft-ch! We are not HERE it is out the window I saw it all, ALL OF IT!"

He pulled her away from him, holding her at arm's length. She felt like a beanbag dummy. Her eyes shone with a dark, horrified intelligence. Her mouth moved, opening, widening, clamping shut.

"THE ATTIC WINDOW!" she screamed and then the trickle coming from her nose gushed to a river. Her ears began bleeding and her screams became the gibbering of the mad. He was a doctor, he was her father, and he wanted to help her, *needed* to, but all he could

do was stare at her, shocked fear bracing his body, his mind spinning.

He leaned back against the stair railing, clutching at it with shaking hands. Sadie grabbed her shock-white hair and yanked, her face contorting, drool slobbering down her face mixed with blood. One of her hands went to her eye and clawed at it, blood seeping through her small fingers. She spun around in circles, tearing her hair, screaming those fricative, nonsense syllables. Peter wept, his eyes wide open, unable to absorb this maniac horror that had been his daughter.

Suddenly, one of her small feet tripped over the other and she plunged down the stairs. Halfway to the living room, the gibbering stopped and Peter knew at once she was dead.

Both of them, he thought calmly, almost serenely. *Both of them dead and I couldn't save either of them.*

He stood at the top of the stairs, looking down at his daughter's crumpled body. He hoped she was at peace.

Doctor Peter Frakes turned from the stairs and slowly began to walk down the corridor. From behind he heard Knowles voice: "Oh, Lord, not again." Then, "Peter, where are you going?"

He didn't call. He spoke. "To the attic, of course."

* * *

The pull-string on the trap door hung down a little lower than normal. Peter glanced at the floor and saw faint tracks that could only have been made by someone pulling a chair across the rug. Sadie, getting one of the chairs up here so she could pull the string, then studiously putting it back so she wouldn't get caught playing in the attic. Peter cursed himself for not noticing these things earlier. Could he have saved her then? Could he have saved Ellie if he had noticed her markings earlier? It was too late to decide now. He pulled the string and the ladder slid own on casters, connecting with the carpeted floor with a muffled thump. He looked up into the black maw of the attic, and something in his mind itched at him to not go up there. For a moment, he hesitated, part of him wanted to run screaming down the hall, past the body of his daughter, past the housekeeper, get in the car and just *go*. He had the choice, didn't he?

Didn't he?

The moment passed, and he began to climb up.

* * *

It was dark up here. The only light was that which came up from the hallway below. Still, Peter could see enough to know that he was in an empty room, a door at the far side of the room. *Staging area* he thought randomly, and traversed the room on shaky legs. The doorknob he touched felt cold, cold. Abject fear coursed through his veins like electrified blood. He did not want to open the door. But he did anyway.

The door swung outward and opened on a maze of mirrors. Peter looked in, unbelieving, and saw his own terrified face reflected hundreds of times. His asthma, usually very light, threatened to close in on him again, settling around his throat like a noose. This was where he got lost before.

You're still lost, a voice in his mind said. Ellie's? Did it matter?

Behind him, he heard the crash of the ladder sliding upward and the trapdoor slamming shut. At once, his terror-calm broke and he tried to lunge, screaming, back into the first room, the room of the sane. But the door swung back on him, too, forcing him into the maze. Peter fought against it, digging his bare feet into the wood of the floor here, but the door was too strong, too heavy for him to budge back. He was trapped.

He looked ahead, seeing himself in his peripheral vision on either side and one of himself in front. The illusion was terrible, as it had been before, when he had lost himself years before losing his wife and daughter. He walked forward. The mirror-Peter walked forward coming to meet him.

"Stop this," he whispered, jogging a little. The asthma was getting worse now, constricting his chest, making him gasp. Claustrophobia pressed down on him, making him feel small and scared and lost. He jogged faster, turning a corner. Now there were a dozen of him.

"No, no," he muttered, the jog escalating to a run, and suddenly there were Peters everywhere, running scared, bumping into mirror-walls, crying in multiple, huffing and puffing and not wanting to scream and then they all ran headfirst into a reflection and the mirror maze shattered.

The attic window was right in front of him.

He tried to close his eyes but found he couldn't. He walked, eyes scarily wide, to the sill of the window and stared out. Oh, the horror. Oh, the

universe constructed of evil, of horror, of nothing rational and sane, images gamboling in impossible freak shows, an entire universe where two plus two is negative zero and unthinkable horrors feast on creatures that are neither solid nor liquid nor gaseous, a black, black place where mewling insanity is tangible and wide-eyed shock-terror roams free, in this realm of ultimate fear, in this universe constructed of pain and feeding on lunacy, humans cannot co-exist, humans cannot see these twisting shapes of madness for certainty of madness themselves, there is no room for petty humanity here, here there is only the transcendence of horror and the blackness of no flesh.

Screaming, howling into that dark, dark place, Peter thrust his fists forward, plunging them through the window, lacerating his hands. Shaking, mewling, he brought forth a shard of window-glass and plunged it into his eye.

"I don't want...," he breathed, "to *see* any... anym..."

He gasped one last breath and then was still.

From outside, something slithered in.